THE SECRET FAMILY

AN UNPUTDOWNABLE THRILLER WITH A BREATHTAKING TWIST

SL HARKER

PROLOGUE

Dear Mom,

I just wanted to say thank you for being a lying piece of shit. You have got to be one of the worst people to walk the face of this earth, I swear. I don't know how you do it. How do you get up every day and look at your own lying face in the mirror and think it's okay for you to walk around like nothing is wrong. If your outsides smelled like your rotting insides, you'd be chased out of town. Your pretty face and fancy clothes and beautiful home hide an ugliness like no one has ever seen before. You're awful. I hope one day, your face matches your heart.

You've ruined so many lives just by being alive. You've been living a lie, and you think no one knows, you think you've gotten away with it, but I know. I've known for a long time. And every time you smile in my face, I want to smack you right in your lying mouth. One day, the truth is going to come out. You aren't going to be able to go on forever, living your charmed life. You think you have everything under control, but you don't. Because I know. I know what you are! I know who you are! And I know what you did. You can't cover up your stink with that expensive perfume much longer. You know what they say about "what's done in the dark."

The thing about people like you is that you think you're above it all. Consequences can't touch you, right? You've created this perfect life, built it brick by brick. Fancy job? Brick. Loving husband? Brick. Adoring daughter? Brick. Beautiful house? Brick. And on and on. But I'm going to be the one to bring those bricks down. Just you wait. One day, you're going to get what you deserve. That brick house is going to come tumbling down around you. And I'm going to be the one who makes sure it does. I'll be there to assure you get everything you deserve.

Why? Because you're a bad person, and bad people don't deserve good things. It's as simple as that. I'll get my revenge on you one day. You aren't going to be able to continue lying and cheating and being a selfish bitch much longer. It's coming to an end. I hope you've enjoyed it, because it's almost over now. You're not going to be able to ruin any more lives. You won't be able to turn your back on me again, Mother. I'll make sure of it.

1

A light wind rustles a stack of papers sitting on a table, ruffling and tugging at them until the top two peel away and skitter across the red bricks of a restaurant patio.

"Hang on. I'll grab them." I jump up and chase the papers, snagging them by the edges and smoothing them carefully before replacing them with the others. I pick up the stack and slowly shuffle through them.

"Katy, honey, these are really good." I pull out a drawing of a young girl in profile, her head tilted slightly up, the barest of smiles playing around the edges of her mouth. "I'm impressed, sweetie. You've worked really hard on these haven't you?"

She nods shyly.

"You should be proud. Look at the improvement on your shading." I lean over and kiss the top of her head which results in her giving me an alarmed look.

"Dad, stop." Katy blushes, ducking her head and letting her strawberry-blonde hair cover her cheeks.

"I mean it," I say, turning back to the drawings. "You've

come a long way in the past year. I love this." I turn over a drawing of what I recognize is our elderly neighbor on her knees in her flowerbed, an oversized hat covering half her face.

"It's all because of Ms. Rawlings. I'm so glad the school finally found a replacement for our old art teacher. Can't believe it took them almost six months." Katy snags her glass of water and sips. "I was talking to her about a camp this summer. It's at the Governor's School of the Arts. What do you think? Think Mom will let me go? I know it's expensive, but you know, I want to be an illustrator, too."

The warmth of pride blooms within me, and I can't stop the grin tugging my mouth. My little girl, if I can still call a seventeen-year-old *little*, wants to follow in my footsteps.

"I'm sure we can figure out something with the art camp," I say. "I can probably pick up a couple of commissions. And I'm sure Mom will be on board."

Katy jumps up and rounds the table, throwing her arms around my neck. "Thanks, Dad."

I pat her shoulder until she lets go and bounces back to her seat.

She picks up her phone and checks the time. "You know, Mom should be here by now."

Glancing at my watch, I hold back a sigh. Stella is often late, especially when it comes to family functions. Her job in pharmaceutical sales is demanding and tends to take up a lot of her time. But, she's good at it. In fact she consistently wins accolades for exceeding quotas. But this isn't the first time she's been late for a family meal, and I'm sure it won't be the last.

"Wasn't she hiking this morning?" Katy flips over her menu and peruses the selections. "The fettuccine looks good."

"Yep. But if she went up her usual trail, she should be back by now. I bet she had to stop at the office for something." I study my menu for a few seconds before pulling out my phone and dialing my wife. The call goes straight to voicemail.

Katy must notice the look on my face, because she grimaces before saying, "I bet her phone is sitting on the bathroom vanity. You know how she is."

I just nod. For someone who's so successful at work, Stella can be very forgetful in her home life. She often forgets her phone or forgets to take it off silent. It's just part of who Stella is, and we've just learned to joke about it.

"Well, I'm starving," Katy announces. "Can we order already?"

Glancing at my watch one more time, I tell Katy yes and signal to the waiter. Stella won't mind. In fact, if she's in the office, she probably won't show up for lunch at all. *Work hazard*, as Stella always says.

"Yes, let's order."

"Great. I'm going to have to cacio e pepe. Do you think I'm saying that right? Cacio e pepe," Katy repeats slowly before giggling.

"I think I'll have something I have a shot at pronouncing." I laugh. "Lasagna."

"Yeah, but shouldn't that be 'la-sag-na...' not 'la-zawn-yuh?'" Katy asks, a smile playing across her face. Her freckle-spattered nose wrinkles when she laughs, and I'm struck by how young she still is and how much life she still has ahead of her. And I feel sad that Stella seems to miss so much of it because of her job. But now, Katy is debating with the waiter over the proper pronunciation of bruschetta, and I forget about Stella for a while, just thankful that I can spend this time with my daughter.

* * *

"I still have some chemistry to do. Ugh, when am I ever going to need chemistry as an artist? Also, I'm so full all I want to do is take a nap. How can I even think with this much pasta inside of me?" Katy rubs her stomach and gives me a fake frown, eyes wide like a puppy.

"Nice try," I say drily, pulling off my jacket and hanging it on the rack near our front door. "Get that chemistry home-work done, and we'll watch a movie later."

"Okay," she replies and bounds up the stairs, her belly full of pasta seemingly forgotten.

I listen for the slam of her bedroom door before I head into the kitchen.

This morning's breakfast dishes are still in the sink, so I quickly unload the dishwasher, rinse the dishes, and reload it. I wipe the counters and give the floors a once-over with the broom.

When Stella and I first got married, I had dreams of hitting it big with my art. I hoped to become an in-demand animator for a big studio or have my own sold-out private gallery shows. I dreamed of earning Hollywood money so I could settle my family on the coast somewhere. We'd live out our lives getting tanned on the beach while I painted.

That's not quite how things worked out. Truthfully, Stella brings home most of the money. Being a freelance illustrator isn't quite as lucrative as some people think. Coming to terms with Stella being the breadwinner took me a few years. We've settled into a rhythm over the years. I have my home studio where I do my commissions, but I spend most of my time as a house husband, doing the chores, making school lunches, and going solo to most of the parent/teacher conferences. I'm able to see my little girl grow up. I was there for the first steps and words and dances and disappointments. I wouldn't change anything. Well, except maybe having Stella home more often.

* * *

Moving from the kitchen to the laundry room, I quickly get a load running. As I'm breaking down a few delivery boxes that Stella stacked in the corner, the doorbell rings. Briefly, I wonder if it's Stella, if she's forgotten her keys. It wouldn't be the first time. I drop the boxes and head for the door.

Opening the door, I find a man in a brown suit standing on our steps. A uniformed police officer is standing a few feet behind him, his thumbs tucked into his belt and his eyes studying the walkway beneath his feet.

"Can I help you?" I ask curiously. I glance at the street and see a township police car parked at the curb.

"Mr. McConnell?" The guy in the suit squints at me.

"That's me. What's going on?" My heart starts to pound. *There's no way this is anything good.*

Police officers don't show up at your door to give you good news.

"I'm Detective Anderson. This is Officer Jones. You mind if we come in?" He shifts from side to side and clears his throat.

"Uh, yeah, sure. Come on in." I step to one side and wave them in as sweat forms under my collar. "Has something happened?" I ask as I lead them into the living room.

"Mr. McConnell, why don't you have a seat," Detective Anderson suggests. His words make my head swim. The room goes out of focus for a few seconds, and I feel myself sway.

"Yeah, I'll sit." I nod dumbly, dropping onto an ottoman. "What's, uh, what's going on?"

"I'm sorry to tell you this, Mr. McConnell, but... there's been an accident."

"Stella?" It feels like all the air has been sucked out of my lungs, and my wife's name comes out with a squeak. *Don't say it, don't say it, don't say it.*

"I'm sorry. There's no easy way..." He clears his throat. "I'm very sorry to inform you that your wife has died."

2

Something is buzzing, and I don't know where it's coming from. Suddenly, I realize it's coming from my own head. I stare up at two strangers, who have just delivered a kick in the teeth so devastating that they may as well have blown up my house around me, too. The detective's mouth moves as he glances between me and the officer, but I don't hear anything he says. Just snatches.

"Around two hours ago, a dog walker found your wife..."

The buzzing gets louder. I blink, wondering if I'm going to throw up.

"It seems that she fell..."

Someone offers me a cup of coffee, but I don't even respond.

"What we need you to do now..."

Then time passes in a blur again.

"...when you're ready," the young officer says.

"What?" I ask numbly.

The detective glances at the officer and clears his throat again. "We're going to need you to formally identify the body. At the hospital."

"Of course." My voice is wooden. "I'm sorry, but I'm going to have to ask you to leave. My daughter..."

"I understand," Detective Anderson responds quickly. "Here's my card. Just let me know when you're on the way, and I'll meet you there. If you'd like to bring someone with you for support, that's fine. You might want them to drive."

"Right, right." I take the card and shove it into my pocket.

The detective turns and motions Officer Jones to the door. "Please let me know if you have any questions." Then they disappear through the door.

I sit on the edge of the ottoman, listening as the door closes softly behind the officers. The house is quiet, with just the soft background sounds of the washing machine as it runs through a cycle. The buzzing in my head subsides, leaving my temples throbbing. I sit, head in hands, hunched over, tears leaking from my eyes, which are scrunched shut. I stay that way until I hear the sounds of Katy moving around in her room overhead.

Katy. I can't tell her yet, not until I see for myself and make sure the police have the right person. *There's always a chance they made a mistake, right?* That can't be unheard of. It would be a twisted and horrible mistake, but a mistake, nonetheless.

After shoving myself upward, I head to the small half bath down the hall. I scrub my face, clearing away all the traces of tears, and straighten my shirt, smoothing out the wrinkles where I've bunched it between my fists. After making myself as presentable as possible, I make my way upstairs to Katy's room.

I can't do this. I stand outside Katy's door, my hand resting on the edge of the doorframe. Pop music weasels it way around the edges of the door, and I hear Katy talking. She must be on the phone. I take a deep breath and rap my knuckles on the door. It swings open, and Katy is there in the old blue T-shirt she wears when she uses her chalk pastels. Her cell phone is shoved between her chin and shoulder.

"Hang on, Kylie. What's up, Dad?" She smiles up at me, a smudge of green chalk on her cheek.

"Uh, I, uh..."

The words don't come out. Nothing does. Katy's brow wrinkles, and she gives me a worried look.

"I have to run a few errands. I thought maybe you'd like to go to Amber's while I'm out. I'll drop you off."

"Actually, that sounds great," Katy chirps. "Hey, Kylie, I'll call you back." She thumbs off her phone and grins at me.

My heart twists as I stare at her sweet face. I study her plump cheeks and the freckles across her nose, the same freckles Stella hated so much on her own nose, until Katy squirms.

"Dad?"

"Nothing, honey. Just... lost in thought is all. Come on. Grab a jacket, and we'll get going." Turning, I make my way back downstairs. I quickly fire off a text to make sure Amber is home. She responds immediately to say she is. I let out a breath of relief and locate my keys and wallet, shove them into my pockets, and stand, waiting on Katy.

Driving Katy to Amber's takes only a few minutes. Amber is a good friend of Stella's, maybe her best friend. Since they met a few years ago, Amber has become like a part of the family, joining us for holidays, celebrations, and even a couple of family vacations. I've come to think of her as more like a younger sister to Stella and an aunt to Katy rather than just a friend. I'm going to have to tell both Katy and Amber about Stella, so I hope that telling them together will help absorb the impact of what I have to say. I doubt it, though.

I leave Katy at Amber's door, giving her a fake smile as she wiggles her fingers at me in farewell. She's already chattering at Amber about something before the door closes behind her. Before I back down the driveway, I pull out the business card and call Detective Anderson to let him know I'm coming. Then I turn the car toward downtown and drive to the place Katy was born.

It's a tall, grey building I've been to only a handful of times. Katy's birth. The time she fractured her wrist and when I had surgery on my shoulder. While both of my parents passed away a long time ago, they did so in different towns. This hospital is synonymous with my life with Stella and Katy. It's part of our history. Which is why it's fitting that I need to come here to identify Stella's body. In a heart-rending, grotesque way.

I finally find a parking spot on the busy lot. After maneuvering in, I sit for a minute, trying to steel myself for what's about to happen. I have to face a dead body, one that the police say is my wife. I don't think I've ever seen a dead body, not even at my grandmother's funeral when I was a kid. A memorial service had taken place in a cold room with an urn and a framed picture at the front. Then we all went home and ate sandwiches the neighbors had dropped off by the trayful.

My parent's car accident was handled by my uncle when I was a student at college. He'd been the one to do what I'm doing right now. To identify them.

The signs to the morgue take me lower and lower, until I'm in the bowels of the building. When I open the last door, Detective Anderson is waiting for me. He holds out his hand, and I grasp it. It's dry and warm. I shake his hand quickly then shove my hands into my jacket pockets.

"So how do we do this?" I ask. My chin starts to wobble uncontrollably and I mutter a quick apology.

"Take your time, Mr. McConnell. It's all right," he says.

I hastily wipe my nose and pull in a deep breath. "I'm okay." Around me, the walls are blue. I suppose it's supposed to be soothing. Stella liked green.

"It will be quick. I promise you that. You'll be behind a pane of glass so you don't have to be in the same room. All you need to do is look quickly and give us a positive ID. Then we'll talk. I won't keep you long, I know you have a daughter to get back to. I'm sure she needs you." He gestures toward the door.

"Right," I murmur and take a step forward.

The swing door opens and I find myself in some sort of viewing area. It's sterile, its blue walls matching the ones in the corridor. Even though I'm not in the same room, a sharp antiseptic smell makes my nose burn.

After another deep breath, I redirect my attention to the glass. In the center of the room is a metal table. A sheet is draped over a figure lying there.

A man in a paper surgical gown appears out of nowhere. "Mr. McConnell, I'm the coroner," he tells me through the glass. "I'm so sorry for your loss. Whenever you're ready."

I'll never be ready, but I nod my head anyhow. The coroner leans forward and peels back the green sheet.

It's her. Oh my God, it is her. That's Stella on that table. That's her auburn hair and her dark-brown eyelashes fanned across her slightly sunburnt cheeks. There's a scratch on her chin and her hair looks different at the temple, like it's covering up a wound, but otherwise, she looks perfect. My lovely Stella.

I quickly nod and take a step back as the coroner quickly whips the sheet back over Stella's face. I turn away and face the detective.

"What happened to her?" My voice is so harsh with unshed tears that I don't even recognize it. "I... I know she fell.

But..." My teeth chatter, and I can barely say what I need to say. "I don't think I heard... what you said."

"Come on. There are some benches in the lobby. No need to stay here now that it's over," he says as he puts a hand on my shoulder and leads me to the door. "Would you like a cup of coffee? There's a vending machine nearby."

I shake my head and he leads me to the benches to sit down.

"So, Mr. McConnell. Stella was found at the bottom of a ravine. At the trail off Coleman Peak. We haven't found any witnesses. Right now we have no reason to believe this was anything more than an accident."

"And... and it was quick? Her death? She didn't suffer?" I ask.

He hesitates. "We believe she may have died from blunt force trauma."

I shake my head in disbelief. "She looked so... so perfect. There wasn't any blood."

He smiles thinly. Somewhere between my rattling teeth and the back of my pounding skull, I realize Stella had been cleaned up before I arrived. The thought makes my stomach roil. I'm not sure how I keep down lunch, but I do.

"Thank you," I finally manage. "I should... get back to my... to Katy."

"I do need to ask you a few questions first," he says. "I apologize. This is a difficult time but I do need to know where you were this morning up until around two p.m."

"I spent the morning with my daughter in the living room. We were both sketching. I'm an illustrator and Katy is really interested in art, too. Then Katy and I went for lunch at Angelo's Italian. We stayed until around two. Maybe two fifteen." I swallow, trying to find enough saliva to help me speak. "We ordered late because Stella was supposed to join us." My voice cracks but I push on. "Then we went home."

The detective nods. "And Stella liked to hike alone?

"Yes," I say. "Sometimes she went with her friend, Amber, but going alone was a good way for her to decompress. She worked really hard."

"Okay," he says. "Well, I think I've taken up enough of your time. Drive home safe. These stressful events can creep up on you even if you think you're fine. Take it easy, okay?"

"Wait," I say, starting a sentence I'm not completely sure how to finish. "Stella hiked that trail all the time. I can't imagine her falling like that."

"It looks like she may have fallen from a tricky area," Detective Anderson says. "There was another death in the same spot about ten years ago. Even experienced hikers get into trouble every now and then. I'm sorry to say that but it's true."

"Okay," I say, not wanting to talk about it further. Not until I've had time to think, anyway. "I'm going to go to my daughter now."

"All right," he says. "And once again, I'm sorry for your loss."

3

My fingers are numb as I open the car door. I can't imagine driving. But I must. I have no choice. When I pull down the sun visor, my waxy face stares back at me from the mirror. I have to get it together for Katy. She needs me to be strong.

I reverse out of my spot, legs shaking. And then I pull out of the lot and onto the road. The detective was right about me finding someone to come with me and drive. But it's too late now. I let my brain go into an autopilot mode as thoughts rush through my mind.

It saddens me to think that my memories of Stella are going to be tainted by what I saw in the hospital morgue. The blue tinge to her lips. The way her hair fell over a broken skull, hiding the wound.

On the way back to Amber's to pick up Katy, I keep thinking of how I'm going to break the news to my daughter. *How can I tell her that her mom is gone?*

Another thought keeps nagging at me: Coleman's Peak. Stella knows all the local trails well and must have hiked Coleman's Peak hundreds of times. It's not a difficult route, even though it is high up. I picture her on the edge, looking down at the trail below. That must be how she was found so quickly, she must have fallen right down onto the trail below as it snakes up the mountain. *How did she manage to stumble and fall off the trail? Did something distract her? Was there an animal? Did something scare her?*

The niggling of the thoughts lead me down a new route. The idea that isn't fully formed. One I don't want to admit to myself. By suggesting Stella couldn't have fallen, I consider the option that this wasn't an accident. Detective Anderson obviously thinks it is. Surely that should be enough to assuage my worries. It's not like Stella had any enemies. I don't know why my mind goes to those dark places, but it is.

My thoughts are all jumbled, and sooner than I expect, I'm at Amber's. I sit in the car for a few minutes before I muster up the courage to get out. I know I have to tell Katy. I have to tell her now.

I think my knees might buckle when I get out of the car. I'm surprised to be on my feet, let alone walking.

Katy answers the door, a smile wreathing her pretty face. It throws me off, I expected Amber.

"Hey, Dad!" she says. Then her smile fades when she takes me in. I know what she must be seeing. A pale face. Trembling lips. Tear-stained cheeks.

"Hey. Listen, Katy, I need to talk to you." I shuffle back and forth on the step, my eyes on my feet.

"What's wrong?" She reaches out and grabs my hand. "Dad, you're scaring me."

Amber appears over Katy's shoulder, her hair shoved into a bun, a mixing bowl in her hands.

"Come on in, Peter. We're making cookies." She uses an elbow to point toward the kitchen. Then she truly seems to see me and her eyes narrow. "Are you all right? You look white as a sheet." She backs away into the hallway as I step into the house. Mutely, I follow her and Katy to the kitchen.

"Dad, what's going on?" Katy watches me, her eyebrows pinched together.

"There's no easy… I don't know how to say this, Katy." I twist my hands together, trying to figure out how to say what I need to. Finally, I just blurt it out. "It's your mom, honey. She had an accident. She's gone."

The bowl slips from Amber's hands and hits the floor. There's a clang as the metal spoon bounces against the tiles. Cookie dough mixture spills out but no one bothers to clean it up. Katy stares at me, her mouth opening and closing wordlessly. Her eyes roll back. I catch her just before she hits the floor.

My knees buckle and I half collapse with my daughter. Once her eyes open again, I wrap my arms firmly around her shoulders. She's shaking uncontrollably. A high-pitched keen rips through the air, and I don't know if it's Katy or me. I feel a hand on my back and glance up to see Amber with huge tears dripping off her chin, spattering down the front of her red blouse. Her other hand rests on Katy's head. I feel a flash of gratitude for Amber then, for the fact that I haven't had to be alone while telling Katy about her mother.

The three of us remain on the floor for what feels like hours. Finally, I manage to get Katy up.

"I'm so sorry, Peter," Amber says, pulling me into a tight hug. "You're both welcome to stay here for the night. I can cook you something."

But I shake my head. "I need to get Katy home." Then I sigh. "There's a lot to start sorting out." Moving onto the practical side makes me taste bile at the back of my throat, but there's no point denying it. And I'll need to be at home to begin everything.

Amber helps her into the car, shutting her door softly after she fastens her seat belt.

Amber makes her way to the driver side and leans through the window to kiss me on the cheek. "Let me help you and Katy. Anything... Ask me for anything, and I'm there. I loved Stella so much."

I nod and wipe tears off my cheeks. "Thanks," I say gruffly. Then I back down the drive and head home.

Katy is asleep before we even leave the driveway.

Without question, this has been the hardest day of my entire life. I've lost my partner, my love. And now, it's just the two of us—just me and my Katy, alone together.

4

"Donna, why don't you sit down for a bit." Peering over the top of the laptop, I pull off my reading glasses and rub my nose.

Donna, Stella's seventy-year-old widowed mother, is wandering around the kitchen, wiping clean counters and moving cups she's already moved three times. Katy is curled into a chair at the opposite end of the table from me, her legs tucked under herself, her face stormy as she studies her phone.

I waited until this morning to tell Donna about Stella's accident. I didn't want to tell her last night then leave her alone all night to grieve alone. Katy and I have been here since early this morning. I've been on the phone with both the funeral director and insurance agency, trying to plan a memorial service for Stella while Katy sits and withdraws deeper and deeper into herself and Donna wanders around the house, touching everything and muttering "oh dear" every so often.

"Hmm. Oh dear. I'm just going to... um, put these towels away." She picks up a stack of kitchen towels she's folded and refolded several times. I watch as she refolds the towels again.

"Why don't you make me and Katy a cup of tea," I say gently. I hope that giving her a task might make her feel less helpless. I know that's how I feel right now.

Her face clears slightly, and she nods briskly. "Yes," she replies, "I think all of us could use a cup of tea. I'll get us some made." Her movements are sharper now that her mind has something to do. She bustles around, filling the kettle and pulling out a tin with an assortment of tea bags shoved haphazardly inside.

Katy's drooping eyes turn to me. I tilt my head toward her grandmother, and she nods slightly before leaving her seat and joining her grandmother at the counter.

"Let me help you, Gran," she says. "Maybe we could find some cookies, too. None of us has had breakfast yet." Katy gives her grandmother a wan smile and reaches into the cabinet above her head to pull out a cookie jar shaped like a cowboy boot. I watch them both as they drop tea bags into cups and arrange cookies on a plate before I turn back to the laptop and try to work on an obituary for Stella.

I consider what I can tell people about Stella that they don't already know. She was supportive and loving, even if her job kept her away from us several nights a week. She and I were able to provide Katy with a solid middle-class upbringing. Well, that's mostly Stella, if I'm being truthful. But I never resented her for it. She was an avid hiker. She was a good friend. She loved her job. Wow, I always end up back at her job. That, more than anything, was the defining factor in Stella's life. Her job came before almost everything. Frustrated, I close the laptop with a snap. Maybe I should give the funeral director the basics and let him fill in the rest of the details. Right now, I really don't have the capacity to write an essay on my wife's life. I shove the laptop away and scrub my eyes with the palms of my hands. Having barely slept last night is catching up with me.

"Here, Dad." Stella deposits a cup of tea and plate of cookies in front of me.

I thank her and sip the tea, my mind twisted with a million thoughts of Stella, hiking trails, and how I'm going to have to raise Katy alone now.

Katy and I spend the rest of the day at Donna's. I leave only long enough to meet with the funeral director and sign a couple of documents. I offer our guest room to Donna in case she doesn't want to be alone, but she waves me off.

"I'm an old woman, Peter. Grief isn't new to me." She gives me a kiss on the cheek and pulls Katy into a tight hug before sending us home.

Being away from her relentless pattering around the house is something of a relief. But the house isn't as warm and welcoming as it used to be. Now there are pictures of Stella to remind me that she's gone. Her socks are in the washing machine. The book she never finished rests on our bedside table. I'll forever walk these rooms and wish my wife was still with us.

Maybe Katy feels it, too. Because as soon as I open the front door, she bolts for her room.

"Katy, what about dinner?" I call after her.

The only answer I get is a slammed bedroom door. Maybe she just needs time alone to process her thoughts without interference. I'm willing to give her that. But I need something to make me feel normal, so I head into the kitchen and start making roasted chicken breasts and salad that neither one of us will probably eat. Now I understand Donna's earlier twitchiness.

I check the chicken, turning it over and giving it another

dousing with some olive oil before shoving the pan back into the oven. Turning my attention to the head of lettuce on the cutting board, I grab a knife and start slicing it into ribbons. Just as I toss the pieces into the colander to wash them, the doorbell rings. The colander slips out of my hands and drops into the sink with a clatter. My heart thumps so hard that I hear it in my ears.

I don't want to answer the door. Yesterday, at almost the same time, our doorbell rang, and the most devastating news I've ever gotten came after. I don't want to answer the door, but the bell rings again. I listen for Katy coming down the stairs but hear no sound. So I walk to the front of the house and stand in front of the door, my hand on the knob. Finally, I snatch the door open.

A man I don't know stands in front of the door. He has dark hair and looks roughly my age. A teenage boy stands next to him, shuffling his red Converses back and forth, his hands shoved deep into his pockets.

"Can I help you?" I ask.

The man just stares at me for a few seconds. He pulls his shoulders back and clears his throat. "Were you married to Stella McConnell?" The question comes out harsh and belligerent. The man's eyes narrow, and his mouth tightens as he crosses his arms over his chest.

"Who are you?" I take a step back, unnerved by the clenching of his fists and the way he leans slightly forward. His eyes are narrow, almost spiteful, as he looks me over.

He sighs, but his body remains rigid. "Were you married to Stella McConnell?" he asks again.

"Yes." I clear my throat. "I was. Unfortunately, she passed away recently."

The speed with which the man's face falls is astounding. Every ounce of bravado and anger drains from him and is replaced by a look of pure pain. The young boy beside him stops his nervous shuffling and stares at me, his lips pressed thin.

"Who are you?" I ask him again. "What do you want with Stella?"

"I... I... Umm." The man stumbles over his words. Finally, he reaches into his pocket and pulls out his wallet. He produces a photo from inside and holds it out to me.

Taking the photo, I flip it over and see it's a picture of Stella. A young boy sits on her lap.

I glance up at the man and back at the photo. "I don't understand. Why do you have a picture of Stella? And who is..." I realize the boy in the picture is a younger version of the boy standing on my porch. "Who... Who are you?"

The man reaches out and takes the picture from my trembling hands, looking at it briefly before he answers me. "I'm Andrew Ritchie. I'm Stella's husband."

5

The words hit me like a gut punch, so hard that I stumble backward. I catch myself before I fall and bend over, hands on my knees, breath rasping in and out in harsh bursts. Spots swim in my eyesight. I shake my head, trying to clear it. When I'm sure I won't fall over, I stand up. The boy glares at me, his eyes narrow and mean.

Is he Stella's son? How? How could it even be possible? He's around the same age as Katy. I do get lost in my art sometimes, but I'd never miss something like Stella being pregnant. No way can this be true. It's absolutely ridiculous.

"You're lying," I blurt. "It's not possible. My Stella would never..." I stop. *Would she?* "How?"

"She lied to us all," Andrew says with a shake of his head. "I don't know how to... I know this is hard. I think we need to talk."

No way do I want this man and his son in my house, not with what he's saying about Stella. *But that picture...* I can't deny it's Stella, and I can't deny it's the boy in front of me, on her lap. I see it now, the freckles, the upturned nose, the auburn hair. I see the resemblance to Katy.

"My daughter..." I gesture vaguely toward the house.

The boy finally speaks. "There's a daughter?" He turns to his father. "Dad, let's just go."

"I need some answers, Theo." He turns to me. "We should talk."

"As long as Katy doesn't come down. She's had enough shocks this week." I glance at the boy, Theo. "Sorry. I guess you have, too." He just shrugs and follows his father through the open door. I glance at the ceiling, willing Katy to stay upstairs, to keep her headphones on. "Just to your right."

I point toward the living room, which we hardly ever use. We spend most of our time in the family room off the kitchen. But now, twice in the past two days, I've escorted strangers into this room, who keep showing up and changing my life with their words.

"Let's keep this as brief as possible," I say.

This man, Andrew, takes a seat on the blue sofa Stella and I picked out together, and Theo settles in beside him. I take the matching chair opposite, putting the coffee table between us.

"So," Andrew starts, "I guess what we need to do is figure out which of us was first. You have a daughter, you said. How old?"

"She's, ah, seventeen."

A look passes between Andrew and his son.

"What?' I ask.

"I guess that answers that." Andrew says with a sigh. "You met her first. Theo is only fifteen."

I don't know why I feel a sense of relief at his words, but I do. Something is satisfying about knowing that I was first. Katy and I came first. At least, we did for a while.

"I don't understand, though," Andrew says, "there's still

not much difference in their ages. When is your daughter's birthday?"

"March," I reply, "but I don't see how... Oh." A thought begins to dawn on me. "When did you meet?"

"September, same year Katy was born, I'm guessing, given Theo's age." Andrew leans forward. "It didn't take her long to get pregnant again, did it?" His implication is clear.

The words hit me in the chest, and I bristle, my jaw clenched so tightly that I can feel it tic. He's baiting me, and I get it, but I won't react. Crossing my arms over my chest, I sit back and level a look at him. Theo is beside him, shifting in his seat, a smirk on his face as he regards me.

"Wait, that's..." I stop and do some quick calculations in my head. "It's impossible. When Katy was around one, one and a half, Stella... She, well, she had a miscarriage."

My heart sinks. I remember it all so clearly. Stella's white face as she returned from the hospital. She'd been out of town and she hadn't called me. I'd been devastated, but I saw the expression of agony on her face when she explained what had happened. I hadn't wanted to cause her any more pain by asking too many questions.

But she didn't, apparently. I wonder what else Stella lied about and considered how much I'm willing to tell this man, who claims my wife was his. *How far will I go to get answers? How far will he?*

"I think it's time for you to go now." Standing up, I point toward the front door. "I think we're done here."

"No, I want to know how she kept the pregnancy, kept Theo, from you. Are you that stupid that you didn't notice?" Andrew stands up and rounds the table. "How did she do it?"

It dredges up more painful memories. A few weeks after the miscarriage, Stella grew so mired in her own grief that she couldn't take care of Katy and couldn't work. She'd haunted our house at all hours, not sleeping or eating, just sitting and staring at the walls, her mind lost in a world I couldn't see. Finally, after some discussion, she decided to check in to inpatient care at a psychiatric hospital in a nearby town. She'd stayed there for almost five months.

Five months. Long enough to have the baby and spend a few weeks at home with her newborn. I remember her coming home, how she launched straight back into work. But there'd been a rocky patch where she'd barely let me touch her. I'd thought it was because of the miscarriage, that looking at me brought her pain. But she was healing.

"She never lost the baby," I murmur to myself. "It's you." I look at Theo, standing slightly behind his father. "She planned it all so carefully. After the fake miscarriage, Stella had a breakdown. A fake breakdown." My shoulders slump. "I helped move her into that hospital."

"What hospital?" Andrew asks.

I clear my throat. "A psychiatric facility. I packed her a bag and drove her there. I guess... I guess she checked out and..." My eyes drift across to the man on my sofa. "Then stayed with you for the rest of the time."

"She was crafty—I'll give her that," Andrew says. "Didn't you ever want to visit her?"

"Yes, but she told me... She said not to bring Katy to that place, that she didn't want her to see her mom like that. She said I reminded her of the pain of losing the baby. We spoke on the phone, though, every day."

I remember waiting impatiently every afternoon for what Stella said was allocated as "phone time." She told me she could use the phone only between noon and two. And all that time, I took care of our daughter. Alone.

Andrew lets out a low, disbelieving laugh. "I was at work during the day. I bet that's when she called you."

"That's right," I say.

His nod is slow and thoughtful. "We could compare a lot of notes, you and I. I'm sure we'll find many occasions like this."

"Stella was so clever," I say. "She always had an excuse right there on her tongue when we were invited somewhere we didn't want to go. And the way she stood up for Katy whenever her teachers overstepped."

Andrew laughs. "And for Theo, too."

My eyes widen as it hits me. Stella attended parents' evenings for Theo. She changed his diapers and brushed his hair. She did all that and somehow managed to look me in the eye and tell me she loved me.

Andrew must notice my expression because he lets out a long sigh. "Peter, I think we both got taken for a ride. But I'm having a hard time figuring out which one of us had it worse."

Something inside me snaps and I realize I can't take any more of this. It's too much.

"It's time for you to go." I rise from the chair. "I don't mean to be rude but I need to process this."

"That's fine," Andrew says. "At least we know why the police didn't tell us about Stella's death."

"How did you find out?" I ask.

"The local news," he says. "It mentioned that Stella left behind a loving husband and daughter."

I shake my head. "That's awful. I'm sorry."

"I think we both have a lot of thinking to do. Just... do me a favor. For now, don't tell anyone else about this. I'll tell Katy when I think she's ready. It's too much right now, planning the funeral and everything."

"That's another thing," Andrew says. He doesn't make a move toward the door. "The funeral. My son lost his mother, too. I can't let you just bury her without acknowledging Theo.

It wouldn't be right for him to miss out on the chance to properly grieve his mom."

I know he's right. This isn't Theo's fault. The kids are innocent in whatever game Stella played. She would have won it, were it not for her accident, but now, we've all lost.

I nod. "All right. Let's stay in touch. We can do this together."

As soon as I say the words, my chest tightens. It's an invitation to let this man and his teenage son into my life. Into Katy's life. But what else am I supposed to do? I believe him. All this time, as I made a life with Stella, I knew deep down that something was a little off. But I never allowed myself to poke at that feeling because our life was happy. And now the Band-Aid holding it all together has been ripped away, leaving the mess uncovered.

I have no choice but to deal with it.

6

"Together," Andrew says. "Good. So Theo will be recognized then? And I will have some control over the funeral?"

Theo looks between his father and me, his face no longer hard but dazed. I don't think it's registered with him until just this moment that this is real. His mom is really gone. His mom really had another family. She lied to him, lied to us all, for years. His face falls, and tears form in the corners of his eyes. He turns away quickly to wipe his eyes. I turn back toward Andrew to give the boy a few minutes of privacy.

I sit back down. It's clear Andrew has no intention of leaving just yet. "I think, since Stella was here in town when it happened, that, well... maybe I should take care of things here. There are already friends and family members here who know about it. It would be strange to cancel or move the services."

The sound of a footstep overhead stops me. I press a finger to my lips and study the ceiling.

When no other sounds emerge from upstairs, I turn back to Andrew. "Actually, I don't know why I'm asking you. Stella's services will be here, with her family, her daughter. I'm the only person in this room who was legally married to Stella. I'm her next of kin."

Andrew's spine straightens. "You don't think Theo deserves consideration?"

Theo is still turned away, his shoulders shuddering slightly. His father reaches over and puts a hand on his shoulder, but Theo shrugs it away.

"Katy is my main concern right now," I reply.

"And Theo is mine," Andrew says angrily. Red blotches form high on his cheeks, and his fists clench. His breathing becomes harsh for a moment.

"What do you want me to do? Huh? Exactly what is it that you'd like me to do? I'm hanging on by a thread here, man. I'm inches from fucking snapping. So just tell me what you want," I demand.

My face grows hot. I pride myself on being an easygoing type of guy, one who takes things in stride and lets stuff roll off his back. But this, this strange man and his son, in my home, laying claim to my Stella, telling me these terrible things, demanding I cater to some stranger—it's almost more than I can bear. I flex my fingers, and they curl into fists.

Andrew raises his hands to placate me. "We don't have to be like this. Just listen to me. We don't have to be at the funeral. We'll have a separate service in our town for Stella if we need to. I just want Theo to be acknowledged, for people to know he's her son."

"And flowers," he adds. "I'd like to have a spray of flowers, lilies, for—for Stella and me. Lilies are—were—our favorite. She'd plant bulbs in our backyard every year..." His face clouds over with grief.

"I don't even know when the service will be." I sigh and

wipe my forehead. "Her... She has to be released. But I will consider your requests, about Theo and the flowers. That's all I can give you right now." The fatigue of the day sets in, and I slump against the door. "I really think you should go now. Look, I meant it about staying in touch, but I need some space, okay?"

"Thank you for at least considering it. Yeah, we'll go." He puts his hand on Theo's shoulder again and turns him around. "Let's go, son."

"I thought I heard voices." Katy's voice sounds out across the foyer, and I freeze for a minute before turning. She's halfway down the stairs, and I have to wonder what she may have heard. She thumps down the last few steps, her feet bare, and stops at the bottom. "Who are you?"

"Katy, it's nothing. They were just leaving." I nod towards the hall, indicating they should leave.

"Wait. Who are you? You seem really familiar." Katy walks up and stands between me and them, her eyes trained on Theo. "Do you go to my school?"

"You'd really better get going," I repeat. "We have things we need to do."

Theo takes a step forward, his brows pulled together, and his eyes narrow. "You're not gonna tell her?"

My voice drops to a near growl. "It's time for you to go."

I can't let Katy find out this way. She needs more time. But Katy pushes around me and stands in front of Theo.

"Tell me what?" She props one hand on her hip and tilts her head, peering up at him. "Tell me what? Dad?" She turns back to me.

"Come on, Theo, let's go." Andrew grabs Theo by the elbow and tries to turn him around and lead him off the porch.

"No!" Theo explodes. "She should know. I have to, so why

shouldn't she?" He jerks away from his father. "The reason I look familiar—"

"Theo, don't. Please. Katy, go back upstairs." I reach out and give her a gentle push, trying to turn her away from Theo and the bitterness in his eyes.

"No." She lurches away from me. "Tell me." Katy turns back to Theo. "Tell me."

"I look familiar because I'm your brother," Theo says in a rush. "Your mom... was my mom, too."

Katy stares at Theo, an unreadable expression on her face. She lets out a harsh, barking laugh. "You know my mom just died, right? Why are you here playing some kind of joke?" She turns to me. "Dad, seriously, who are these people?"

"Katy." I reach out and put a hand on her shoulder.

"No." She pushes away from me, shaking her head. "I don't believe you. How can... How can that even be true?" Her tear-filled eyes flick between Theo and me. "It's not possible. No. How could she have another kid and you not know, Dad?"

"Sweetheart, it's complicated," I say to her. "Let's go in and talk about it. Theo and Andrew were just leaving." I jerk my head toward the door.

"I don't want to talk!" Katy shouts. "This is stupid and not true. How could you believe them, Dad? They're lying. They want something. It's not true!" And with that, Katy sprints away from us. I hurry after her, watching as she flings open the front door. She flies down the steps and across the yard before I can stop her.

"Katy, wait!" I yell at her disappearing back.

I take off after her, but she's long-legged and in better shape than I am. By the time I reach the end of the drive, she's gone. I don't even know what direction she took.

"I'm sorry," Andrew says from behind me. "We didn't mean to upset your daughter." He sounds genuine at least.

They walk toward their car, parked on the street, and climb in. Theo watches me as they pull away from the curb and drive off.

I turn in the opposite direction and walk a couple of blocks, trying to spy Katy farther down the street. She's nowhere to be seen. I pull out my phone and call her, hoping that she just happened to have her phone on her when she took off. She doesn't even have shoes on.

The phone rings until voicemail picks up. I dial her again and again and leave message after message. "Katy, please come home. Let's talk about this." Finally, out of options, I get in my car and circle the block, searching for a glimpse of her pink sweatshirt.

I drive down our street and cross onto the street that runs behind our house, driving so slowly that a couple of aggravated drivers pass me, gesturing rudely. When I still don't spot her, I drive another street over to the elementary school and check the playground there. I know that sometimes, when school isn't in session, the high schoolers sit at the rear of the playground, under the trees, and do whatever it is high schoolers do when they're together. A group of boys with skateboards slung over their shoulders eye me as I drive past slowly—still no Katy. The sun is starting to set, and she's still not answering her phone. I point the car in the direction of home, hoping she's returned while I've been out looking for her.

"Katy!" I call the second I fling open the door.

She doesn't answer, so I sprint up the stairs and fling open the door to her room—no one. Sitting on the edge of her bed, I drop my head into my hands and suppress the sob that's lodged in my throat. I've lost my wife, and now I don't know where my daughter is.

My phone dings, and I rush to pull it out of my pocket. *Please, let it be Katy.*

I'm fine, Dad. I just need some time.

That's all the message says. She doesn't answer me when I text back to ask where she is and when she's coming home. I can do nothing. Sighing, I go downstairs and sit in the family room, alone in a house that's too big and too quiet for just one person.

7

A stack of photo albums rests on the bottom shelf of the bookcase stacked with board games and funky little art projects that Katy has brought home over the years. It probably should have been cleaned off years ago, but I'm suddenly glad I never bothered to do a spring-cleaning purge. I grab the albums and haul them over to the coffee table. Next on the list is a nice, big glass of bourbon. I don't think I can do this completely sober.

The first album is all Katy, from birth until about age twelve. Katy wrapped in a hospital baby blanket, her tiny bald head covered by one of those knitted caps all newborns get in the hospital. There's Katy in a red swimsuit, running through a sprinkler set up in the backyard. Katy's ninth birthday, when she was in her horse phase, her cake printed with prancing ponies.

I check my phone again—nothing since her last text. I desperately want to know where she is, but she is seventeen, so I can't really do anything to make her come home right now. I send her a quick text: *I love you, Katybug. Be safe.* Then I turn back to the albums.

Next is our holiday album. The first picture—Stella on the beach with her head tossed back, her mouth open in a laugh —nearly undoes me. The pain that slices across my heart is so intense that it nearly stops my breathing. Grabbing my glass, I take a burning gulp and wipe a hand across my mouth.

As I flip through the pages, I'm suddenly struck by the thought that none of our trips were more than a few days long. We never took a vacation over four days. Stella always said she was needed at work, that she couldn't take off more than a few days at a time. Now, I know the real reason. She couldn't justify that much time away from her other family, her secret family. *Or was that us? Were we the secret family?*

Angrily, I take another gulp of my bourbon, the ice clinking against my teeth. I thought about the way she always planned our trips, our day outings, where we'd go for lunch. I thought that was just her type-A personality, but it was her making sure we didn't accidentally run into Andrew and Theo. And I'm sure she did the same with them, planning everything around keeping us a secret from them. My entire life has been a lie, my entire marriage a sham. My wife wasn't mine alone. Part of her belonged to strangers. *And who got the best part of her? Was it Andrew? Was it me? Did she love Theo more than Katy? Did she really love any of us at all?*

I don't even realize my hand wrapped around the glass until I fling it across the room. It hits the wall, and bourbon and ice spray across the room, soaking the carpet in the pungent, smoky liquid.

"Shit." I push the albums away, and they tumble to the floor.

A single photo comes apart from the heap of albums and lands near my foot. I reach down to flip it over. It's one I've never seen before. I quickly flip open the album from which it escaped and look for the spot it came from. There are no empty spaces in the album. The only place I think this picture came from is where the plastic cover has come away from the book. The more I look at it, the more I think Stella secreted this photo away. She didn't want me to see it, but she wanted it with her other keepsakes and memories.

I examine the image. A baby is wrapped in a blanket, but it's not Katy. I don't think it's Theo either, as the picture appears to be too old. It's grainy and slightly out of focus. It's hard to tell, but the baby looks newborn. I turn it over, but nothing is written on the back.

I'm not sure I can cope with one more revelation. In a fit of frustration, I shove the picture back in the album and haul the pile back onto the shelf.

* * *

After the photos and cleaning, I pour myself another glass of bourbon and check my phone again to see if I've missed a message from Katy—still nothing. I send her a text message to let her know I'm here when she needs me. Walking around the house, I touch the things that belonged to Stella: the throw she liked to snuggle into while we watched TV, a scarf left hanging by the back door, her favorite coffee mug, even some unopened mail addressed to her. All these little things let me know that, yes, Stella was real and that she lived here with me and Katy. But I can't help but wonder about her other life, her life with Andrew and Theo. *Did she have a favorite mug there? What did her kitchen look like? Did she leave toothpaste splatters in the bathroom sink there? Did she use old receipts as bookmarks like she did here? Was she a different person with them, with him?*

I swirl the bourbon in the bottom of my glass before throwing the last of it down my throat as I stare out from the patio doors into the backyard. Stella's hydrangeas will bloom soon. She loved to float the periwinkle-colored blooms in a white bowl in the center of our dining table. But she told Andrew she liked lilies. Maybe she invented a completely different character with him, like she was split into two separate people. And if she did, it was the invented character Andrew made love to and argued with and did all of those things couples do.

But who am I kidding?

As I stare into the yard, wondering if I should get rid of the red Adirondack chairs Stella hated so much, my phone rings. I snatch it out of my pocket.

"Katy?"

"No, hon, not Katy. It's Donna." Stella's mom's voice echoes through my phone. "Why isn't Katy with you?"

"She... uh, just needed some time alone. But anyhow, did you need something?" I make my way back into the kitchen and study the bourbon bottle on the table, wondering if I should have another drink. *To hell with it.* I pour another inch into my glass and sip while I listen to Donna talk about song arrangements for Stella's funeral service.

"Hmm, yeah, that sounds fine," I mutter, not really recalling what she's said. "Listen, Donna, we have to talk about something." I might as well get this out while the liquor is loosening up my tongue. "I don't even know how to tell you this, so I'll just come out and say it as plainly as possible. Stella had another husband. And child."

"What?" Donna lets out a small laugh. It's a nervous sound, almost like she knows what else I'm going to say.

"Yeah, I've had a visit from them, her husband and son, this afternoon." I wash down the bitter taste in my mouth with more bourbon before I tell Donna about my encounter with Andrew and Theo.

"Oh, Stella, you selfish, selfish girl," Donna says sadly. "I really should be more surprised, but I'm not. Stella always did what she wanted, when she wanted. Even as a young girl. I'm sorry, Peter. I guess this is partially my fault."

"Donna, no. If you didn't know, how could any of it be your fault?" I've wandered around the family room, phone to my ear, but I finally settle on the sofa and put my drink down. "I'd be the last person to blame you for this."

"Fred and I both worked when she was a child and sometimes, I wonder if she got the attention she needed." Donna's voice cracks, like she's living in her own regrets. "I could've told you more about Stella before you got married. She, you know, she was a sweet girl, but when she turned sixteen, things changed." Rustling sounds come through the phone line, as though Donna is taking a seat, getting comfortable for what she wants to tell me.

"Okay. Nothing unusual about that, I guess. Kids do change as they get older."

"This was different, though. I saw such a change in her, physically as well as mentally. She'd lost some weight, you know. She was chubby as a child, but it fell off as she hit her teens. After that, well, she started shoplifting. And lying. She lied about everything: little things, big things." Donna goes quiet for a few moments. "I'd never met a person more untruthful than Stella. She lied even when she didn't have to. I figured that's what made her so good at her sales job. She was able to tell people what they wanted to hear, not what they needed to hear. She's always been manipulative. I guess I thought when she married you that it would all be okay. That you and Katy would help her settle down. I never thought she'd do something like this." Donna sighs. "I'm sorry, Peter."

"You have nothing to apologize for. But there's something I need to know. When Stella was in the hospital for those months, you know, after she lost the baby, did you ever go see her?" Picking up my glass, I twist it, watching the light play off the amber liquid inside.

"Oh my God, I'd almost forgotten about that. Certainly hadn't thought about it lately. No, I never visited her, though I begged to. I was so worried about her being in that place for so long." There's a pause. "Oh, she didn't." The truth is audibly dawning on Donna. "Oh, the baby. She never lost it. It's the boy, isn't it?" Her voice catches. "I've had another grandchild all these years, and she never... I just didn't know." She's crying now.

"Please, don't. There's nothing we can do about it now. All we can do is figure out how we're going to move forward from here. And that includes Andrew and his son, I guess." I sigh and put the glass down, pushing it away.

"But that's just it, Peter. How do you know that the boy isn't yours? She was obviously with both of you. It's not outside the realm of possibility." Donna sniffles.

"Yeah, I guess it's not." I pick the glass back up and drain it. Something about that suggestion makes me feel uncomfortable. I think about Theo and his intense, staring eyes. "Listen, I have to go. I'll talk to you again soon about the service. But you contact me if you need anything."

"I will," she says. "Take care."

Then I sit with my empty glass in my empty house and ponder the idea that Donna could be right. Theo could be my son.

8

Dear Mom,

So you're dead. Good. I'm glad. I know most people would be shocked to hear me say that, but I am. Especially since I know what kind of person you were. You were a bad person. You've lied and cheated and manipulated everyone and everything around you, just so you could get your way, and to hell with everybody else and their feelings. Right? I'm right—you know I am.

You know, I think the world is a better place without someone like you in it. You're a bad person, Stella. Sneaky and conniving. A horrible mother and wife. Did you really think you'd be able to get away with it? With any of it? I mean, I guess you did. Things have always worked out like you've wanted them to, right? I guess you had no reason to think any differently this time. Must have been nice to be you for a while. I can't think of another person who's managed to arrange their life like you have. Did it ever get tiresome, though? All the deceit and the play-acting? All the secrets? Oh yeah, I know your secrets. I know all of them. How did you ever get through the day with the weight of what you did on your shoulders? How did you look into the eyes of the people that you claimed to love and lie, lie, lie over and over again. Hmm?

I think I've finally come to the conclusion, though, that not having a mom is better than having a mom like you. You treat people like they're your own personal toys. You've built up your own personal dollhouse, haven't you?

You know what? I'm glad it was me. I'm glad I'm the one who finally got to show you what retribution is. That my face was the last one you saw before I pushed you off that cliff. And you know what else? I smiled when I heard you scream, and I smiled when I heard your body hit the rocks. I swear I could hear the crunch of your bones as they broke. And I hope it hurt. I hope you felt it all before you died. Because no matter what, the pain you felt was nothing compared to the pain you've put people through all these years. I hate you, bitch. And I'm glad you're dead.

9

"Dad?"

Katy shakes my shoulder. I groan and roll over, almost falling off the sofa in the process. Through bleary eyes, I see Katy standing above me. She studies the empty glass on the table. When I finally manage to shove myself into an upright position and peer up at her, she just raises an eyebrow at me.

"You okay?" I croak out. Clearing my throat, I try again. "I was worried about you last night."

"Yeah, it sure looks like it," she replies with a pointed glance at the bourbon glass. "Anyhow, yes, I'm fine. Sort of. Or at least whatever 'fine' means now. I'm not physically hurt, you know."

"Want to talk about yesterday?" I don't ask her where she's been. I'll let her tell me when she's ready.

She sighs, and it's long and deep, and I can tell she thinks whatever she has to say is going to hurt me.

"It's okay. Say whatever you want," I tell her. "I doubt there's much you could say that would shock me any more than I already am."

"How am I supposed to feel, finding out my mom is nothing but a big, fat liar. She's lied to us all these years, Dad." Katy shakes her head as a disgusted look crosses her face. "She didn't love me. She didn't love either of us, or she never would have done it."

"That's not true, Katybug. Your mom loved you." I don't know what else to say to her, how to make her feel better about finding out that her mother betrayed us all. But I know Stella loved Katy. She was her mother, after all. And I'm sure that Stella loved Theo, too. What kind of parent doesn't love their own child? Honestly, I'm afraid to know the answer to that.

"Yeah, right." Katy rolls her eyes and turns on her heel before stomping off into the kitchen.

I hear her banging around, slamming cabinet doors and rattling dishes, and not long afterwards, the scent of freshly brewed coffee wafts through the house. With a groan, I heft myself off the sofa. I might have had a little too much last night. Swiping the sleep out of my eyes, I quickly straighten the sofa and grab my glass to take into the kitchen.

"Katy," I say as I deposit my glass into the dishwasher, "we should talk about this."

"Nothing to talk about. There's coffee." She points needlessly at the coffeemaker.

"Come on, sweetheart. I know you're hurt," I say, grabbing a coffee cup from the nearby cabinet. I pour a cup and heap sugar into the liquid. "Thanks for this"—I hold up the cup—"but I still think we should talk."

"Dad." Katy faces me with a sigh. "Seriously, I don't want to talk about it anymore. What good is it going to do? Mom did what she did. And yeah, maybe she did love us, all of us, on some level, but what good does it do to know that now? She left us all in a mess. Me, you, and her other family." Katy stops and shrugs. "Let's just deal with the funeral services. We'll figure the other stuff out later."

"That's very mature of you."

Leaning against the counter, I sip my steaming coffee and watch Katy drop slices of bread into the toaster. My heart contracts. My poor baby girl has had to grow up far too quickly in just the past few days. We were just talking about art camp, and now she has to deal with burying her mother. I can't even begin to fathom what it must be like for a girl to lose her mother. I've always been and always will be here for Katy, but for some things, a girl just needs her mom. I don't understand all the intricacies and nuances of being a woman, of having to navigate this world in a woman's body. I can't help but ache for Katy because I'm becoming acutely aware of all the things she's going to miss out on, not having a mother. No mom at graduation or dropping her off at college. No mom to help choose a wedding dress or to be there when Katy finally has a baby of her own. Of course, I'll be there, but it won't be the same.

"Mmm," Katy mumbles at me.

Our conversation appears to be over. I pour more coffee into my cup and take a seat at the breakfast table. My head is throbbing. I probably need water and some Tylenol, but I just gulp my coffee, wincing when it burns the top of my mouth. As Katy scrapes butter onto her toast, a knock comes at the door.

I glance through the window of the side door and see Amber, Stella's friend, standing there with a bag in her hand. Jumping up, I unlock the door and usher her inside.

"Morning," she says, depositing the bag on the counter. "I thought you two could use some breakfast." She looks around and tuts. "You need more than toast and coffee. I know neither one of you has eaten well." She unloads the bag, pulling out containers of pancakes, sausages, and bagels.

"Morning, Amber." Katy drops her toast and opens a take-out container of pancakes. She pulls the top one out, rolls it up, and bites into one end.

"Really, Katy? Get a plate, please, and a fork." I shake my head at her, though Amber just smiles and pushes the sausages closer to Katy with a wink.

"So, how is, you know, the planning going? Anything I can help with?" Amber piles up a plate of food and deposits it in front of me before refilling my coffee cup. She bustles around, comfortable in our space, dishing out food and sweeping the empty containers away.

"Thanks for the offer, but I think I have everything under control." I bite into a sausage, chewing thoughtfully. "There is something, though." I glance at Katy. "You're Stella's best friend, so I have to ask. Do you know Andrew and Theo?"

"Who?" Amber blows on her coffee and shakes her head. "Doesn't sound familiar. Co-workers?"

"Uh, not exactly." I glance again at Katy, who stops eating and pushes her food around her plate.

"Go ahead, Dad. Tell her. But I'm not staying to hear it again." Katy stands up, her chair squealing as she pushes it away roughly. She glances between me and Amber before stalking off, leaving her plate of food on the table.

"Katy!" I call after her.

In a moment, her bedroom door slams overhead.

"Let her go," Amber says. "She needs some time." She walks over to the table and lays a comforting hand on my shoulder before taking away Katy's unfinished plate. "I'm always here if she needs to talk."

"I know. And I'm thankful she has someone like you she

can lean on. It's just... A lot has happened in the past twenty-four hours." I push away my plate and lean back in my chair.

"And it has something to do with this Theo and Andrew?" She comes back with the coffee carafe and refills my cup.

"Yeah." My voice is morose. I stare into my coffee cup before lifting it and taking a sip. "I guess. I don't know how to say this, really, so I guess I'll just come out with it. Stella had another family—a secret family."

Amber drops heavily into the chair opposite mine, shaking her head like she's confused. "A... what now? A secret family? What are you talking about, Peter?"

So I tell her everything I know about Andrew and Theo, everything that happened yesterday, when they showed up at our house and dropped this bomb. I tell her everything Andrew said. I tell her about the picture of Stella and a young Theo. And when I finish, I'm drained but somehow relieved that I have another person to share this burden with.

"I can't... I just can't believe it," Amber says, her voice shaking. "I never would have guessed. It sounds almost impossible, being able to hide something like that for so long. Stella was full of secrets, wasn't she? And what do you know about this Andrew guy?"

"Almost nothing, except that we shared a wife," I say, a bitter edge to my voice.

"Well, let's remedy that right now." Amber disappears into the family room and comes back with a laptop cradled in her arms. She slides it onto the table and drags a chair closer to me. She settles in and boots up the laptop.

"What was his name again?" she asks, bringing up a browser.

"Andrew, uh, Ritchie." I inch closer and peer at the screen.

Amber types in his name and scrolls through the returned searches.

"There." I point at a picture that has popped up. "That's him."

"Okay, let's just..."

She clicks on the link, and a page pops up: Harbor Light Books. A picture of Andrew is there, with a paragraph underneath. She leans forward and reads the page.

"Well, he owns a bookstore. Or rather, a couple of bookstores. Looks like he does quite well." She turns the computer toward me, which I read quickly. "Let's check out his Facebook."

She clicks over and quickly locates Andrew's social media page. It has pictures of Andrew and Theo in restaurants, on a sailboat, and getting ready to zipline into a leafy green jungle canopy. *So many pictures.* Stella lived this whole other life.

"No Stella, though," I murmur as I click through the pictures. "Never any Stella. She didn't even have social media. And there are no pictures of her on my or Katy's pages." I quickly locate a page of Theo's and click through his as well, seeing typical teenage stuff, memes and pictures of friends. "This explains a lot, how Stella never wanted to be on social media. Said it was because of work, that she had to be careful about maintaining a good reputation. She really just didn't want to get caught." I shove the computer away. "Was everything she did a lie?"

"Hey, hey." Amber pats my shoulder. "I may not have known about her double life, but I do know that she loved you and Katy. Never forget that."

"I'm having a hard time with this, reconciling the Stella I thought I knew with finding out about a Stella I never would've believed existed. It's just going to take some time." Wiping my face with my hands, I lean back in my chair as Amber quickly clicks through a few more pages.

"Well, it was easy enough to find out about their personal

lives online, but I have to ask you, Peter, what about the financial side of things?" She tabs out of Facebook and turns to face me.

"Shit." I mutter and sit up straight. "I never even thought about that."

"Right. We don't know anything about her finances with Andrew." Amber stands and clears the breakfast dishes from the table. "You seriously might want to consider getting an attorney."

"What? Why?" I sit up straight, thoughts beginning to churn.

"Because you need to know who inherits what from Stella's estate. From what I can tell, this Andrew has just as much a claim as you do. What do you know about Stella's financial affairs?" Amber scrapes food into the trash and loads the plates into the dishwasher.

"Very little, if I'm being honest. We had separate accounts. Stella just wrote me a check to help cover monthly bills. You don't think...? I guess she could have had other accounts that she had sent to, well, to her and Andrew's home. Did they have a home together? Do you think?" I slam shut the lid to the laptop and shove it away. "Fuck. This is such a mess. Why did she do this to me?"

"I don't know, Peter. But none of this is your fault." Amber comes back to the table and sits down, grabbing my hand. "Stella isn't who any of us thought she was, but she was still our Stella. Try to remember the good times you had with her, how she was a good mom to Katy and a wonderful wife to you."

"But was she? I mean, honestly, what kind of good wife and mom does this? And not just to us—she did it to Andrew and Theo, too. She lied so she could get what she wanted." I stop and shrug. "I don't know how I'm going to get through this, how I'm going to be able to stay strong for Katy."

"You'll do it for Katy because you have to. And I'll be right here for you both." She pats my hand again before getting up and moving around the kitchen, quietly cleaning up. As I watch her, some of my anger dissipates, and I find my heart lightening.

Amber's right—I'll do it because I have to. I'll do it because Katy deserves the father she can get, now that her mother is gone.

10

"Today?" I ask. "You're closing the investigation and releasing her today? Already?"

My phone rang early this morning, and when I answered, I was surprised to find Detective Anderson on the other end. I hadn't expected to hear from the police this soon.

"Yes, today, or this morning, rather. We'll release her to the funeral director, and they'll pick her up and take her back to the funeral home. I'm assuming you've already spoken with them?" The detective sounds slightly harried, and papers shuffle in the background.

"And there's nothing else you can tell me? About the accident?" Blearily, I make my way to the kitchen and pull a canister of ground coffee from the cabinet.

"I'm afraid not. There weren't any witnesses, if that's what you're asking, but we really don't have any reason to suspect it was anything more than a tragic accident."

I set the coffee canister down with a thump. "Okay. But you do know about her secret family, don't you? Doesn't that change everything?"

"Mr. Ritchie gave us a call after he spoke with you. He was

asking for details on Stella's death. I told him what I knew," the detective admits.

"And what did you think about what he told you? About Stella and him and us." My hand tightens around the phone.

"It's really none of my business, Mr. McConnell. I'm not about to insert myself into your domestic troubles. I just wanted to let you know that you're cleared to set the date for your wife's services."

"I've been thinking about it, and I think it's pretty damned suspicious that Andrew Ritchie showed up right about the same time Stella had her accident. You don't think it's something that warrants looking into?" I didn't realize I'd voiced my suspicions, but here we are.

That Andrew might've been involved in Stella's accident occurred to me last night while I lay in my bed, alone. I'm having a hard time accepting the accident. I keep going over in my mind how often Stella hiked that trail. She was such a careful hiker, usually very aware of what was going on around her. I'd hiked with her before and had a hard time keeping up. And I was always quite surprised by how much of a stickler she was for hiking rules. That she fell seems almost impossible when I think about it.

"Both Mr. Ritchie and his son, Theo, have alibis for the day Stella died. Like I said, it was a tragic accident. Call the funeral home in a bit. They'll give you all the other details you need to continue your planning."

"All right," I say, admitting defeat. "If Andrew and Theo have solid alibis then so be it."

After hanging up, I forget about the coffee and make my way upstairs, stopping outside Katy's door.

"Katy, honey." I knock lightly. When she doesn't answer, I knock more loudly. Finally, I push her door open and step inside.

She's not here. Her bed is made, and her jacket is missing from the back of the chair where she usually tosses it. I wonder how long she's been gone. Pulling my phone out of my pocket, I quickly pull up her number and call. It goes straight to voicemail, as usual lately. *Shit.*

I call Amber.

"Hey, sorry it's so early," I say when she answers.

"No, it's okay, I was already up. Something wrong?" She stifles a yawn.

I feel a twinge of guilt for waking her up. "I just wanted to know if you've seen or heard from Katy this morning."

"I'm afraid I haven't. Is everything okay?" The sleep clears from her voice as I picture her sitting up in her bed.

"I don't know, really. She's made a habit of disappearing and not answering her phone ever since Andrew and Theo showed up." I stop and scrub my fingers through my hair. "I don't know what to do."

"You have to let her grieve in her own way, Peter. She'll come around eventually and realize she needs you. Till then, just be patient with her." Amber's voice is soothing, and I find myself relaxing.

"You're probably right. And she's practically an adult. It's not like I can really stop her from leaving the house. I just wish she'd let me know she's okay every now and then. A text would be nice." I circle back downstairs into the kitchen and consider the coffee canister I left on the counter. "Just so I don't worry."

"I know, I worry about her, too. But listen, I'll talk to her, okay? Try to convince her to at least keep in touch with you when she feels the need to take off. But give her some space."

"Yeah, okay. I will." I drum my fingers on the coffee canister.

"Let me know if there's anything I can help with," she says.

"Thanks, I will."

I hang up and finally decide against the coffee. I want something stronger, but it's definitely too early for bourbon. I'll wait until at least twelve. For now, I'll go find something pretty to bury my wife in.

* * *

Stella's closet is close to immaculate. Her suits are hung neatly, arranged by color, with matching shoes lined up underneath. I know without opening the dresser drawers that her lingerie is arranged the same way, carefully folded and color coded. I always marveled at her fastidiousness, and now I wonder if she was just trying to keep everything in check, making sure that none of her life with Andrew bled over into ours. I push the thoughts aside and rummage through her dresses. The blue wraparound was a favorite of hers, so I pull it out and put it aside. And she always looked lovely in the green, so I pull that one out, too. The hanger slips out of my hand, and when I bend over to retrieve the fallen dress, I notice a small box pushed all the way back into the corner, behind her coats. It's just peeking out, and I never would've noticed it if I hadn't dropped the dress. I push the coats aside and grab the edge of the box, pulling it toward me.

Dresses forgotten, I sit on the floor of her closet and pull the lid off the mystery box, noticing as I do that it has no dust on the top. She kept it clean, then. The first thing I see inside is a small pile of clothes. As I lift the pieces out, one by one, I notice most of them still have the tags on. And they seem young, childish, not something Stella would wear. They also seem to be out of style. I pile the clothes to one side and reach into the bottom of the box, and my fingers skim something made of hard plastic. As I pull it out, I see that it's an ID. A driver's license. I flip it over to find a much younger version of Stella staring back at me. Studying the date, I realize it's a fake license. Stella is no older than sixteen in the picture, but the ID puts her age as twenty-one. No one gets a fake license to vote, so it's pretty obvious Stella was a wild child in her youth. I think of all the things her mother told me, how Stella lied all the time and did what she wanted. Shaking my head, I toss the license back into the box and feel around again, next pulling out a piece of folded-up notebook paper.

It's a letter, and it's in Stella's handwriting. It's old, dating from the time of the ID if I'm right. It's not addressed to anyone, but the contents pull at my heart. In it, Stella talks about how much this person hurt her. She sounds devastated, which makes me sad, seeing her anguish poured out onto a page that obviously never reached the intended recipient. I have to wonder who the person was and why they would hurt Stella so badly. The page is creased and smudged, which makes me wonder how many times over the years Stella pulled this letter out and read it. Knowing she was reliving whatever made her write this letter makes my throat tighten with the threat of tears. I fold the paper and shove it back into the box along with the clothes and ID. I replace the lid and place the box back into the corner and collect the dresses I've chosen to bury my wife in. And as I make my way back downstairs, dresses draped over my arm, I realize that I know very little about the woman I married, the woman I've spent the past twenty years with. Suddenly weary, I sit on the bottom step and cry, my tears falling heedlessly on my dead wife's funeral clothes.

11

KATY

The trail is empty. I climb upward, my thighs beginning to burn from the effort. I'm not a hiker like my mom was. She loved being on the trails, pushing her body hard up the inclines and wiping the sweat off her forehead with a grin. The views weren't the reason she walked. She didn't care about seeing sweeping mountain vistas or glittering ocean views. She hiked hard trails just so she could say she did. She wanted to be the best at whatever she did, selling pharmaceuticals or taking on the most strenuous trails. The defined calf muscles were just an extra goodie for her. That's why I'll never understand how she fell. Mom didn't make mistakes.

It's why I want to see where she fell.

I push up the trail, sweat starting to bead my brow. *Damn, I should've brought a water bottle.* Oh well, I'm not going all the way to the top, just to the spot where it happened. Then I'll turn around and go back down. I don't think I'll die of dehydration before then. I keep heading up the narrow dirt track, dust pluming behind me with every step.

There's a *crunch* behind me. The unmistakable sound of a shoe on dirt.

I spin on my heel and peer down the trail. I've just rounded a corner, and the thought that someone might be lurking behind the curve spooks me and sends a shiver up my spine. *Don't be stupid, Katy,* I tell myself, *this trail is open to anyone.* I turn back around and start heading up again.

After another fifty feet, I again get the distinct feeling that someone is behind me, but when I glance over my shoulder, all I see are trees and boulders. I shrug it off and keep going. I'm close to the spot where it happened.

The clearing opens up the side of the trail, a "scenic over-look" they call it. It's about halfway up the mountain, a spot for people to take a rest, drink some water, and look at the valley spread out below them. I cross the clearing and stop a few feet from the edge of the ravine, too nervous to get any closer. Leaning forward, I try to peer over the edge without moving any closer than I have to. A twig snaps behind me. I spin, my heart thumping so hard that I can hear the whoosh of blood in my ears. A figure is walking across the clearing, the shadows from overhanging trees obscuring the person's face. They approach, and I see it's a man—no, a boy. It's that boy who came to my house, who said my mom was his mom, too.

"It's Theo," he calls out.

That's right—Theo. He stops a few feet away and shuffles his feet in the dirt.

"Are you following me?" I ask him, suspicion setting in.

"No, not really. I just happened to be here, to show up when you did. I guess you didn't hear me call you in the parking area. Katy, right?" He steps forward a bit. "I'm your brother, I guess."

"Yeah, I guess you are," I say.

I don't know where else to go with the conversation. Are we just supposed to immediately feel like family? Because right now, Theo is just some guy who happens to be my brother. And I don't like the way he's looking at me. His eyes are sly. I step to the side and shuffle myself away from the edge a bit more. I don't know that Theo wasn't here when Mom died, that he wasn't angry at her and pushed her. No, I can't think like that. And my face must have given away my thoughts because Theo steps back and shakes his head.

He stays silent for a few moments before finally asking, "Do you want to look over, you know, where Mom was?"

Mom. This strange boy called her mom. I don't know what I expected. It's not like he would call her Stella or something. It's just so bizarre, hearing him say "Mom" and knowing that he's talking about my mother—our mother, I guess. This is still something I can't wrap my head around. And I don't know if I want to. I'd be happy if this guy just disappeared and I didn't have to know about him. But I guess he could feel the same way about me.

"I don't think... I don't know. I don't think I want to see it."

I step back just as Theo steps forward. His arm brushes mine, and I snatch mine away like I've been seared by a brand. Theo continues until he's at the edge of the clearing, his toes playing along the edge of the drop.

"You should step back," I say, my voice strangled. I picture him slipping, tumbling down to the bottom of the ravine, trees scratching at him, his head bouncing off the rocks that litter the slope—just like Mom. "Please, step back."

He peers at me over his shoulder, something unreadable in his dark eyes before he finally shrugs and takes a couple of steps backward. "Better?"

"Yeah, thanks." Unease slips between my shoulder blades like a knife, and I turn away from Theo and head back toward the trail.

Coming here was a mistake. I don't know what I was thinking about, what I thought I might find by coming to the place my mother died. Nothing is here for me. The trees aren't going to give up any secrets about the day my mother fell. When I'm about fifty yards down the trail, I hear footsteps running up behind me.

"Hey, wait," Theo calls.

I don't want to stop, but I do anyway. I guess it's the least I can do. He catches up and walks beside me as I begin my descent to the trailhead. Neither one of us says anything for a few minutes as we walk. Finally, Theo decides to speak.

"Listen, I know it's strange. This is something that I've never heard of before, secret families. It's like something from one of those bad movies on cable, you know? There's no one else who knows what it's like, no one except you and me."

I shove my hands into the pockets of my jacket and keep walking.

"I'm just saying I think we could help each other, maybe. Like, get through this. You don't have to be mad at me—I didn't do anything. I'm just as innocent in this as you are. I didn't ask for this, and I know you didn't either. We should at least try to get along."

I stop walking and look at Theo. I can see my mom in the curve of his jaw and the shape of his lips, which is strange. And we share the same spatter of freckles. He's right, though. Neither of us asked for this. It had nothing to do with us and everything to do with what my mom did, what she hid from all of us.

"Okay," I say finally. "Maybe it won't be so bad. We can

help each other, I guess." I pull out my phone, ignoring the texts from my dad. "Give me your number."

So on the trail, we exchange numbers. Afterward, with a grin, Theo says goodbye and takes off down the trail at a run. When I reach the bottom and look around the parking area, he's gone.

12

"Are they late?" Donna fusses around the kitchen, folding and refolding a tea towel someone left on the counter. "They're late, aren't they?"

"Relax, Donna," I say. "They won't start without us."

Donna, Katy, Amber, and I are in the kitchen, waiting on the car service to pick us up and take us to Stella's funeral service. Donna has spent the morning alternating between silent tears and bursts of nervous energy. Amber has tried her best to soothe us all, making coffee and offering pastries someone from Stella's office dropped off the night before. Katy is sullen, sulking in one of the breakfast table chairs.

"They're not late." Amber gently extracts the towel from Donna's trembling hands.

She sets it aside and puts a hand on Donna's shoulder, leading her over to the table and easing her into a chair.

"I'm not going," Katy announces abruptly. She stands up, pushing back her chair with a screech. "This is stupid, anyhow."

Donna lets out a gasp and begins to fan her face.

"Katy, honey, of course you're going. You can't miss your mother's funeral," I say softly.

"Why? It's not like she'll know," Katy replies, a hint of venom in her voice.

"That's not necessary," I snap at her. "You're going. End of discussion."

"Fine." She flops back into her chair and crosses her arms over her chest. She refuses to look at me.

Amber murmurs softly to Donna, helping her into a sweater, and Katy still hasn't spoken by the time the cars pull up. Standing, I brush imaginary lint from my black suit and clear my throat. Amber helps Donna, who has started to cry softly, from her chair and leads her to the front door. Katy stares at me, her mouth set in a stubborn line, before finally getting up with a huff and following them out the door. I'm just a few feet behind. At the top of the porch, I stop and watch as Katy, Amber, and Donna make their way to the first car, behind the hearse, like a trio of ravens in their mourning clothes. Katy peers from the corner of her eye at the dark vehicle carrying her mother. I can't imagine the emotions running through her young veins and I don't blame her for the outburst. It's taking every ounce of willpower to stop myself doing the same.

Amber reaches the car first and opens the rear door, ushering Donna in, with Katy following behind. I sit in the first row of seats with Katy by my side. In front of us, I glumly watch Stella's coffin, feeling oddly numb about it all.

When we've gone only a few blocks, Katy speaks up. "Dad, why is there an empty car behind us?"

"I meant to tell you—" I start. Then I shake my head slightly. "Actually, you've been avoiding me so I haven't been able to tell you. It's for Andrew and Theo."

Before she can react, the car glides to a stop in front of a hotel. Outside it are two figures dressed in black.

Katy snorts in indignation behind me. "You have got to be kidding me," she huffs.

"Sweetheart, I felt like it was the right thing to do." My mouth is suddenly dry, and I wonder if I really have done the right thing.

"Did you ever think of asking me? Or how I might feel about it?" She turns her head and stares out the window. "You know half the town is going to be there. How am I supposed to explain to my friends who these people are?"

"You don't owe anyone an explanation, especially today," I reply.

Andrew and Theo pass our car, and Andrew tips his head slightly at me before they make their way to the car behind us.

"Oh, is that them?" Donna leans forward to peer out the window, trying to catch a glimpse of the Ritchies as they walk by.

"We can worry about them later," Amber says. "For now, let's focus on getting through this day together. Katy, honey, I know you're brave. You can do this, okay?"

Katy doesn't respond. I try to take her hand but she pulls away.

I let out a shaky breath and face forward as the car glides away towards the church. Hot anger bubbles up from my insides. Stella's lies have robbed me of grieving for her. I just want to get this day over and done with. I sense there will be no catharsis for me today. No moment of closure where I can say to myself that I've bid farewell to my love.

A small crowd of people stands on the church steps as the cars pull up to the front. A few familiar faces break away from them and make their way to the hearse. Some friends and work colleagues of Stella's have agreed to serve as pallbearers, and they wait to speak to the funeral directors. I step out of the car and a few yards down, Andrew and Theo do the same.

The steps clear of people, everyone heading inside to wait for the service to start. The hearse driver opens the rear door and steps back, allowing the pallbearers to pull the casket from the back. Gingerly, the eight men balance it on their shoulders and make their way slowly, step by step, up the stairs and into the nave. I follow them with Katy and Donna just behind me. I hear a muffled weeping as I lower my head and follow the glossy white casket into the church and down the aisle.

She's in white, like the first time I watched her walk down the aisle. She promised to be my one and only for life. But it was a lie.

After what feels like a walk to the gallows, we finally reach the front and take our pew. Katy, Donna, and Amber slip in first, and I follow, taking the aisle. When I take my seat, I feel someone standing at my elbow. I look up to see Andrew and Theo standing next to me. When I give him a small negative shake of my head, his face clouds before he turns and directs Theo to the pew opposite ours.

Funeral flowers clog my throat with a sickly scent. My head buzzes, blocking out the sounds of the congregation settling down for the service. And then I space during the eulogy, my mind floating as I tune out, willing my consciousness to anywhere but here, to any universe where I'm not burying my wife with my motherless daughter beside me. I only vaguely hear the priest's prayers, the Psalms read, the hymns sung, a poem recited by a woman from Stella's office. All of it is just a tumble of words that don't mean anything to me. Throats clear around me, and people cough into their fists. Donna sobs at the end of the pew. Katy has her head buried in her hands. Amber sits silently with huge tears pouring down her cheeks. She doesn't wipe them away.

I hear a half-hiccupped sob and turn my head. Andrew and Theo are across the aisle, but that's not where the sob came from. Theo, in fact, is simply staring straight ahead. There's no expression on his face other than a look of slight boredom. His eyes are dry. He reaches up and scratches his ear.

Andrew, though, is gazing right at me. His expression sears through me like he's trying to peer into my brain. I shift uncomfortably and bring my eyes back to the priest. A few minutes later, I glance across the aisle again to find Andrew still glowering at me. His eyes are dark and his jaw tight as he studies my family. I turn away and drape my arm over Katy's shoulder and pull her close, like I can protect her from whatever thoughts are churning behind Andrew's stormy eyes.

13

Several uneventful days pass after the funeral and that moment of catharsis never comes. Now that the planning phase is over, I don't have anywhere to direct my energy. I alternate between wandering the house at all hours and sleeping in intermittent fits on the sofa. Sleeping in the bed I shared with Stella is too hard. I consider moving all my things into the guest bedroom but haven't had the energy to make the move.

I shuffle outside to the mailbox, still in the grubby sweats and T-shirt I've been wearing for a couple of days, and I pull out three days' worth of piled-up envelopes. The next-door neighbor calls out to me from where he's weeding his zinnias, but I don't stop to talk, just flap my hand in his direction instead and shuffle back inside. I drop the mail on the foyer table without sorting through it and head into the kitchen.

Amber is here. She's been coming over early every morning and staying until late in the evening. She's practically moved in. I can't say anything, though, because she's cleaned and cooked for me and Katy even though neither one of us eats very much. Amber serves up meals and snacks every day and cleans up the barely eaten remains afterward. She even offered to help me start organizing Stella's things for donation. Though, I can't face that just yet.

Amber brings over a cup of peppermint tea and sets a plate of cookies at my elbow. I thank her even though I'm not hungry. I pick up one of the cookies and take a bite. My mouth is dry, and the cookie crumbles unappetizingly. With a grimace, I wash it down with the tea before pushing the plate away.

"You need to eat something, Peter," Amber says, her voice cajoling. "You've lost weight since the funeral."

"I'm fine," I say testily. Then I sigh and try to smile. "Sorry. I don't mean to be short. I'm just so tired." I gulp some of the tea to appease her.

"It's fine. And I know it's going to take time. You'll get through this, Peter. I know it doesn't seem like it now, but time will help. I know—platitudes," she says with a quiet laugh. "I don't think anyone really knows what to say to a person who's grieving, but I think it's true. Time will help." She quickly sweeps the crumbs into a napkin and tosses it into the trash.

"You're right. Of course you're right. I just need... I don't know what I need, really." I toy with the cup in front of me.

"I know what I need." Katy's voice echoes across the room as she steps into the kitchen.

"Katybug, come have some tea. There are cookies." My hand searches for the plate I pushed away just a few moments ago.

"That's okay, Dad, I'm not really hungry." She crosses the floor and drops into the chair opposite mine. "I think it's time I went back to school."

"Oh." I sit up straighter in my chair. "You don't have to, you know. You can take a few more days off. We've got clearance from the school. We can have assignments sent home if you'd like."

"No, I need to get out of this house. I hate it here." Katy pulls the plate of cookies toward herself and pushes them around with her finger. "Thanks," she says as Amber puts a cup of tea in front of her. "No offense, but this place is a morgue. I can't be here every day, all day anymore."

"Well, you're not, really. You've been going out a lot," I point out.

While it's not something I want to push with her, she has been leaving the house every day, staying out until late evening most days. She doesn't mention who she's been with or where she's been going. I worry, of course. Anybody would, with what we've been through recently. But even Amber agrees that Katy needs space and that she'll come to me if she really needs me.

Katy just shrugs and bites at her thumbnail.

"Fine, you can go back to school if you think you're ready. But no one is going to think less of you if you need more time. You've been through a traumatic event," I say. "We both have."

"What support group did you get that from?" she snipes at me.

"Why are you getting snippy? I said you could go back to school," I reply, annoyance making my voice tight.

"Then, thanks, I guess." She stands up and walks out of the kitchen.

Before long, the front door opens and closes.

"And there she goes," I say sadly. "And I said the wrong thing as usual." I sigh. "At this point I'd be happy if she got some help elsewhere. Like a support group or something. Do you think there are any around here? Maybe I should look into a therapist."

"It's definitely something I'd keep in my back pocket. For now, let her take the time she needs." Amber settles in at the table with her own cup. "I think there's something else we need to talk about, too."

"What's that?" I push the teacup away, get up, and cross to the refrigerator, where I pull out a cold bottle of beer.

"Peter, it's not even noon," Amber says, a slight note of disappointment in her voice.

"I don't care." I crack the cap with a whoosh and take a deep pull off the bottle before I settle back into my chair. "What did you want to talk about?"

"I think you should go see an attorney about Stella's estate," Amber replies.

I think about it for a few moments, sipping on my beer. Amber is right. I should get an attorney to help settle the estate. Throughout the funeral-planning process, I hadn't even thought about settling her affairs afterward. Stella told me she'd set up life insurance, but now that I come to think about it, I don't remember her ever producing the paperwork so who knows. She did own half this house, though. Those are the assets I know about. For all I know, there are hidden accounts I know nothing about. And unless she has a will stating otherwise, most of her estate would probably go to Katy. And Theo.

"You're right. I need an attorney," I say firmly. "I just don't know about Andrew," I say half to myself.

The darkness in Andrew's eyes play on my mind more often than I care to admit. The way he looked at me during the service gives me goosebumps. He hardly spoke to me that day. After the internment, Andrew and Theo left, and I'm sure it led to plenty of gossip. The two of them sitting at the front of the church, Andrew staring at me, Theo with his bored, dry eyes. What kind of people are they, that they didn't express any emotion at the funeral of someone who's supposed to be important to them?

"What about him?" Amber chooses a cookie from the plate and dips it into her tea before taking a delicate nibble.

"Is he entitled to anything? I know my marriage to Stella is the legal one. But does living with her half the time all these years entitle him to anything?" I twist my mug in my hands.

"That's a very good question. If Stella didn't leave him or Theo anything, do you think he has grounds to contest her will, considering Theo is her son?" She drops the cookie and dusts the sugar off her hands.

"I'll make a few phone calls this afternoon—see if I can find someone. But there's something else. And I need you to tell me if I'm crazy for this. Don't hold back if you think I'm being ridiculous." I tap my fingers nervously on the tabletop.

"What is it?" Amber sounds concerned. She reaches over and stills my fingers.

"It's something I've been thinking about. I want to have a DNA test done. On Theo. I have to know if he could be my son."

Amber studies me for a few moments. "You sure about that? That's a whole other can of worms you'd be opening by doing that."

"It's just something I can't shake. What if he is? Stella was obviously sleeping with us both. What if she didn't even know?" I swallow against the pain in my gut, thinking about my wife with another man, with Andrew Ritchie. "I need to know."

Amber blows a long breath out and raises her eyebrows. "Wow, what a mess Stella left behind. Okay, yeah, you definitely need an attorney. And a damn good one."

14

The house is quiet in a way that's almost unsettling. Katy went back to school this morning, so no footsteps sound overhead, no muffled pop music comes from her room. Amber has gone back to her place. She says her plants are going to be angry at her for neglecting them. So I'm the only one here, wandering around downstairs with a cup of coffee in my hand that I'm not actually drinking.

I take the stack of mail from the foyer table into the family room and sort through it while I let a piece of toast go cold on my plate. None of the mail is important—mostly junk, a couple of bills, a few condolence cards. I throw those away without reading them. Maybe it's childish but I'm done grieving for this woman and reading platitudes about a liar.

After a few minutes of spacing out on the sofa, I decide I should probably get dressed. I take my now tepid coffee and cold toast to the kitchen and dump them before I head upstairs to change out of the basketball shorts I've worn for three days. Without even realizing, I find myself slipping into the well-worn jeans and an ink-stained T-shirt from art school that have served as sort of a working uniform for me.

Since I'm dressed the part, I decide the best course of action might be for me to try and get back into doing some work.

My studio has sat in darkness since Stella's passing. My heart hasn't been in it. But I hope that when I open the door and the scent of ink, paint, and paper greet me, the familiarity of it all will spark something that will lift some of the darkness pressing in on me daily. I push the door open, flick on the light, and wait. Nothing.

I force myself into the room and over to the windows, where I push up the blinds and let light flood the space. Dust spins through the sunbeams. The place could use a good cleaning. My drafting table is covered in a series of sketches I'd started working on the week of Stella's death. They're simple, drafted in charcoal, but they feature Katy and Stella set in a cartoon world as a couple of superheroes. They're flying over buildings, capes billowing behind them. In another frame they stand with their arms akimbo and their chins tilted jauntily. I thought they were cute at first, mother and daughter superheroes, but now the sight of them tightens my chest with rage. I snatch the sketches up, crumple them, and toss them into the wastebasket.

With nothing else to do, I sit on the stool in front of my desk, set up a blank piece of sketch paper, and choose a charcoal pencil. Without any thought as to what my subject might be, I start sketching. The pencil glides across the page. A few jagged strokes in and the illustration takes form. I soon realize I'm drawing Andrew. Tossing the pencil aside, I turn away from the desk, pissed at the heat building in my cheeks.

I can't help myself. I pull out my phone and navigate to Andrew's social media accounts. I find his Instagram and scroll through. It's a picture-by-picture sketch of the last few years, and many of the photos are of Theo: Theo playing Little League, blowing out birthday candles, making faces at the fish at an aquarium. Theo and his father. *Did Stella take that picture? And is he really Theo's father?*

I zoom in on Theo's face, searching his features, looking for something familiar. *Stella's freckles and hair are there, yes, but what about his jawline? Is it similar to Andrew's? Or to mine? What about the straightness of his eyebrows, the way his cheek curves? Are those my earlobes?*

Damn you, Stella! Damn you for all you've done, for all you've put two families through.

Did she think she'd be able to get away with this forever? That she'd outlive both her husbands? What was she going to do once she no longer had her job to blame her absences on? And how dare she put our kids through this? I wish she'd just, I don't know, just cheated on me. She had an entire life, though, that she hid, that she lied about. She missed so much of Katy's life by being a part-time mom. And I'm sure the same could be said of Theo.

I pull up another picture of Theo. I don't know how I'm going to approach Andrew about this, but I really think, for all our sakes, that we should have a DNA test done. It's the only way to know. I know there's no way Stella would have been able to say for certain if me or Andrew is the father. The logistics simply weren't in her favor. She was sleeping with us both. And I know—as much as I tell myself that it's for the kid—I know that I have purely selfish reasons behind wanting to find out. After the look Andrew gave me at Stella's funeral, I'd like to knock him down a few pegs. Not very evolved, I know, but it's true.

I've even had the thought that maybe Stella couldn't handle her own subterfuge anymore, that maybe her accident wasn't an accident after all. While I'd like to think Stella wouldn't have been capable of something like taking her own life, she hid so much from me that I can't say for sure. So if I found out that she'd purposely tumbled down the side of that mountain, I wouldn't be shocked.

As I scroll through more pictures, the phone buzzes in my hand. I fumble, caught off guard, and almost drop it before I'm finally able to answer.

"Hi, Mr. McConnell, this is Ms. Baker at the high school."

The clock shows me it's just past lunchtime. Hours passed while I was absorbed in the Ritchies' lives on social media.

"Oh, yeah. Hi, Ms. Baker. Is there something wrong?" My heart speeds up as I think about something happening to Katy.

"Well, I hope not. It's just that Katy left school today without being signed out. I don't want to make a big deal out of it. I'm willing to give her some leeway because of the circumstances, but I thought you'd want to know." Ms. Baker clears her throat, and the silence stretches between us.

"Oh. Of course, yes. Thank you so much for calling. I'm sure she just felt overwhelmed and is on her way home. Thank you again." I hang up before she can say anything else.

Katy's been disappearing ever since we found out about Stella, but I thought that maybe her wanting to return to school was a sign that she was ready to regain a sense of normalcy. She's lucky Ms. Baker feels some sympathy for her, or she could really have gotten into a lot of trouble. But I've had enough of this "space" everyone keeps telling me to give her. I want to know where my daughter is.

The first thing I do is call Katy, but naturally, the phone goes straight to voicemail. I expected as much. And as much as I don't want to worry Donna, I call her anyway, just to see if Katy might be there. I didn't really expect her to be, so I'm not surprised when Donna tells me no. I get off the call with Donna as quickly as I can, before she has a chance to spiral and suggest reporting Katy as a missing person.

I don't have much luck with Amber either.

"No, I haven't seen or heard from her today," Amber says when I call her. "Do you think we should be worried?"

"I have no idea. But I feel like it's time for Katy to start letting me in. She's been isolating herself far too much." I pace back and forth across the family room, feeling caged.

"Let's go look for her, then," Amber suggests.

I'm immediately on board. "I'll see you in five." I grab my keys and head out the door, impatient to locate my daughter.

15

KATY

With Dad moping around all day, I thought coming back to school was a good idea. But God, I think it's worse here. Everybody keeps staring at me. When I walk down the hall, all I hear are whispers behind me. Everyone in the school knows my mom died, and I'm getting treated like a lab experiment because of it. Teachers keep giving me these sad looks and telling me to take any time I need to finish assignments.

And my friends are even worse. They've been up under me since I walked in the doors. They're always asking how I am, if there's anything they can do. Kylie offered to do all my notetaking in chemistry, and Bailey didn't even want me to carry my own backpack. Even Ms. Baker called me out of first period to "check in" with me and to tell me her office door was always open. *Gag.* I swear, if I have to see one more person look at me with those sad puppy eyes or have another teacher pat my shoulder, I'm going to puke.

So now it's lunch time, and I'm hiding on the far side of the quad behind a pillar with a hand-painted poster announcing the next pep rally. I critiqued the poster for a few minutes in my head then slid behind the pillar and pulled out my lunch. My sandwich tastes like cardboard, but I can't blame anyone but myself for that. I'm the one who made it. I nibble at it, pulling at the crust and dropping it into my lunchbox. When I'm about halfway through, my phone chimes. I roll my eyes because I know it's either my dad checking on me or Kylie asking where I am. I don't feel like dealing with either one of them, so I ignore the phone until it dings again. And then again.

"Dammit," I mutter, pulling my phone out of my pocket. I flip it over and check the messages. It's not my dad or Kylie. It's Theo.

Hey, it's Theo. You free?

I text back: *You want to meet up?*

Green Point Park. I'll be there in fifteen minutes.

I stare at the messages for a few minutes, wondering why Theo wants to meet. I wasn't exactly nice to him the last time I saw him. But then again, I did give him my number. From across the quad, Kylie calls for me. Without another thought, I drop what's left of my sandwich, grab my backpack, and make a quick run for the library. When the librarian has her back turned, I slip out the side door and down the back of the school. Without glancing backward, I take off across the ball fields, cut underneath the bleachers, and come out on the far side. Then I grin. *That was easier than I expected.* I shoulder my backpack and make my way across town to the park. To meet my brother. How freaking weird.

I spot Theo before he sees me. He's on the swings, kicking up dust with his feet as he swings back and forth. I walk up behind him and watch for a couple of seconds before I speak.

"Hey."

He puts his feet down and skids to a stop, jumping off the swing and turning to face me. "Hey," he says back. He's in a black T-shirt with a band name I've never heard of printed across the front and a pair of shiny black boots with lug soles. With the hair falling across his forehead and his nonchalant attitude, he looks impossibly cool, like the frontman of a band.

"Hey," I say again and immediately regret it when he smirks slightly.

"Come on, let's go over to the tables." He grabs a backpack off the ground and moves off. "You coming?" he calls back over his shoulder.

"Yeah." I follow him to a covered pavilion with picnic tables arranged underneath.

He jumps up and sits on one of the tabletops. I follow more slowly and carefully set my backpack to the side. I don't know what to say to him, so I just sit silently and watch him from the corner of my eye. He digs around in his backpack and pulls out a bottle of water, which he offers to me.

"Oh, no thanks," I say even though I am pretty thirsty.

With a laugh, he takes a large gulp from the bottle, grimaces a bit, then offers it to me again. "It's not water."

"Oh." Slowly, I reach out and take the bottle from him. As surreptitiously as possible, I wipe the top and take a quick sip. The liquid tastes like rubbing alcohol and burns my tongue. I cough and pass the bottle back.

"Vodka," he explains and takes another sip. "It's not the good stuff. Dad keeps that under lock and key, but whatever... It does the job."

"What job?" I ask as he hands the bottle back. I take another drink, bigger this time, and manage to keep myself from gagging.

"The job of helping me keep my shit together."

"Yeah, I could use some help with that myself," I mutter,

then take another sip. "Is there a reason you wanted to meet?"

"Nothing particular. Just figured with Mom gone..."

"Stop," I tell him, standing up and hopping off the table. "I don't want to talk about her. And it's weird hearing you call her 'Mom.'"

"Well, it's who she was. What else am I supposed to call her?" He takes the bottle back. "Sit down."

"Don't tell me what to do," I say, bristling. I don't know why I came here, but it wasn't to fight with this guy, my supposed brother. But I find myself climbing back onto the table and sitting beside him.

"I'm not. But like I said, I just figured you were probably tired of all the bullshit, too. I know I am. Everybody treating me differently at school and Dad constantly checking in on me. He's even suggested therapy," Theo says with a harsh laugh. He nudges my knee with the bottle, and I take it again.

"Yeah, same, same," I tell him. "Well, except the therapy thing. My dad hasn't said anything about it. Yet. I know it's coming, though." The vodka starts to go down a lot more smoothly.

"The trick with therapists is just figuring out what they want to hear. It's really not that difficult. Don't worry, if you have to go, I can coach you through it. I've been to plenty of therapists." Theo leans over and bumps his shoulder against mine.

"You'd do that?" I ask.

"Sure, why not?

"I don't know. We barely know each other." The world starts to soften around the edges, and I feel light.

"I feel like I know you better than anyone else in the world right now. How many people can say they've been in a situation like ours?" He smiles at me for the first time.

"Exactly. I know what you mean. There's no one else who can understand this, what I'm going through. I mean, how am I supposed to tell my dad that I'm so angry at my mom that I'm glad she's dead?" I laugh a little and hiccup.

"Well, I'm here. And I get what you're saying. I'm pretty pissed at her, too." He shrugs.

"You don't seem like it, you're so... I don't know, calm. How do you do that?" I lie back on the table and fling my arms over my head. "Teach me," I say with a laugh.

Theo bends over me, so close our noses are almost touching. "It's something you can't teach, sister. You're born with it, or you're not." He plants a wet kiss on my forehead. "But don't worry about a thing. We'll figure it all out."

"You reckon?" I say. I hiccup again.

He nods.

Feeling better, I close my eyes and sense him moving away. When I open them again, I'm alone.

16

"Wait. Is that her?" Amber taps my arm and points in the direction of the playground area of Green Point Park.

We've circled the town for the past two hours, and as I was about to give up, Amber suggested we check the park again. And sure enough, there's Katy, sitting on a kiddie swing while dragging her feet through the dust.

"Looks like." I turn the car around and find a spot in the parking area. Amber and I get out of the car and start toward the playground.

"Katy," I call out.

She doesn't look up.

I slide a look at Amber and shake my head. "She's been so angry lately."

"It's one of the stages of grief, you know," Amber replies. "She'll come around to acceptance eventually."

"Sooner rather than later, I hope." We continue on across the grass until we reach the playground. "Katy?"

She finally looks up. And she giggles. "What's up, Dad?

Oh, and of course, Amber. Can't go anywhere without Amber, can we?"

"Katy Ann, are you...?" I step forward and lean over Katy, sniffing. "Jesus effing Christ." I turn toward Amber. "She's drunk."

Amber's eyes widen, and she shakes her head. "Are you sure?"

"Where's the bottle, Katy?" I turn back to my daughter.

She just shrugs. "Don't have it."

"Oh," Amber says, surprise coloring her voice. "She is drunk."

"Come on, Katy." I tug on her arm and help her up from the swing. "We've got to get you home." Amber takes her other side, and together, we half carry Katy to the car and deposit her in the back seat, where she immediately keels over onto her side.

"Is she going to be okay like that?" Amber peers into the back seat.

"She'll be fine," I say tightly.

I can't believe I've just found my seventeen-year-old in a park, drunk, after skipping school. I don't know what happened to the sweet girl from just a few weeks ago, who was excited about going to art camp and looking forward to starting her senior year and applying to art schools. Never would I have thought that Stella's death would change Katy like this. I glance in the rearview mirror and see her balled up on the back seat. She moans. I press my lips into a thin line but don't say anything else until we get home.

"Come on, Katy. In the house." I help her out of the back seat and let her cling to my arm so that she won't wobble and fall over as she walks up the steps.

Amber takes my keys and opens the door for us. I lead

Katy into the kitchen and help her into a chair at the breakfast table.

"I'll make some coffee," Amber says quietly. She moves around the kitchen, filling the coffeepot and scooping grounds into the paper-lined basket.

Katy cradles her head in her arms and moans again.

"Let me know if you're going to throw up so I can grab the waste bin," I say drily. "I don't want to have to clean up puke."

"I'm fine," Katy mumbles from underneath her arms.

"Yeah, you look fine. What were you thinking, Katy? Leaving school without telling anyone and then getting drunk in a public park?" I sit opposite her and cross my arms over my chest. "I don't even think grounding is good enough for this."

"You can't ground me. I'm seventeen," Katy replies, her voice grumpy. "It'd be ridiculous."

"I can, and I will, if that's what I decide," I say. Then I soften my voice. "Why did you do it?"

"I just felt like it, okay? I needed to blow off some steam. And I don't know why you're giving *me* a lecture considering you've been half drunk since Mom died." Her voice becomes muffled. "Could you maybe leave me alone?"

"Absolutely not, young lady. As a matter of fact, I'm going to be keeping a sharper eye than ever on you. I'll take you to and from school from now on, to make sure you're getting there and staying there."

"God, Dad, you're acting like I killed someone!" Katy sits up and pins me with a vicious glare.

"I'm just glad you didn't get hurt somehow. That was a dangerous stunt, Katy Ann."

Amber puts one cup of coffee in front of me and one at Katy's elbow.

"Drink your coffee," I tell Katy. "You're going to need it."

She raises her head and wraps her hands around the steaming cup. When Amber lays a hand on my shoulder and gives it a comforting squeeze, Katy notices and narrows her eyes. I ignore the look.

"So, who got you the liquor?" I ask, taking a sip of my coffee.

It's hot and just lightly sweet. Amber's helped so much that she knows how I take my coffee. I smile up at her before turning back to Katy.

"Well?"

"No one," she says quickly—too quickly. "I got it myself."

"Oh, really? Well, hand over the fake ID, then." I hold out my hand and wriggle my fingers. "Come on."

"I don't have a fake ID. They just... let me buy it," Katy mumbles.

I can tell she's lying to me. Her eyes won't quite meet mine. But if she won't tell me the truth, I can't do anything. There's no way to force an answer from her. Exasperated, I sigh deeply. Every fiber of my being is tired, weary of worrying about Stella and Andrew and Theo. Now, I have to add in an acting-out teenager. My shoulders droop, and I scrub at my face.

"Maybe you should just go to your room for now. We'll talk later, when you're sober." I jerk my head towards the stairs. "Go."

Clumsily, Katy pushes her chair back and stumbles out of the kitchen. She looks back at me like there's something she wants to say, but she just shakes her head and makes her way slowly up the stairs. I listen and hear her door slam shut. Then I heave a sigh of relief. At least I know where she is now.

"She's having a hard time," Amber says, taking Katy's seat. She reaches across the table for my hands. I let her take them, enjoying the warmth in her slim fingers as she covers my hand with hers. "Go easy on her."

"I just don't know what to do. There's not a handbook for what to do when your wife dies and has a secret family in another town, you know. This is new ground for me."

"I think this is ground that's been covered by very few people," Amber says with a small laugh. "But I know you will get through. You and Katy will come out the other side, stronger than ever."

"And what about you? I know you loved Stella, too. You were very close. I guess no one ever thinks about checking in on the best friend." Amber's hands are still on mine, so I don't move. It feels like it's been a century since I've been touched.

"Oh, don't worry about me," Amber replies. "I'm just happy being here with you and Katy and being able to help where I can. Speaking of which, I'll make you dinner tonight."

"You don't have to," I tell her. "I'm sure you have things to do."

"I don't mind. Besides, my houseplants aren't exactly the best company. And they'll survive an evening without me." Amber stands, heads to the refrigerator, and rummages around inside. She pulls her head out and tuts at me. "I'll go to the market for you guys tomorrow. There's an appalling lack of decent food in here. It's all funeral casseroles."

"You've got to love the bereavement food," I say with a forced grin. "I've been meaning to toss those."

"No worries. There's enough stuff here for me to whip up some pasta. I'll get the rest sorted tomorrow. Maybe while you work?" Amber sticks her head back in the fridge and pokes around until she finds some tomatoes and butter. She bustles around the kitchen, humming softly.

Having someone want to cook a meal for me is nice. Stella left all the housekeeping and cooking duties to me, and I thought I didn't mind, but watching Amber makes me realize what I may have been missing out on. Stella always came in from work just in time to eat. Sometimes she even disappeared into her office soon after to do even more work. Sure, she brought in the money, but I'm realizing now, watching Amber, that I didn't have much of a partner. I had a financier —whom I shared with other people.

"Hang on. Let me help you."

Amber smiles at me and nods, so I pull bread out of the pantry and start spreading butter across the slices to make garlic bread. Amber and I work well together, passing bowls and spoons, laughing softly, and one of us bumps into the other one. And for a while, I forget about Katy, and I forget about Stella and Andrew, and I just enjoy being with a person who seems to enjoy being with me, too.

17

Dear Mom,

Well, here we are again. Me talking to you and you not able to answer. That's about par for the course for us anyhow, right?

I thought it's what I wanted, that you being gone would fix all my problems, but it's not happening the way I thought it would.

Honestly, I thought everything would be better once you were gone, that I'd be able to get on with the life I deserved without you in the way. But somehow, I feel bad. I don't know if it's because you're dead and I'm the one that did it or because of how you left everyone in the lurch. I mean, seriously, you fucked up a lot of people pretty bad. So why, then? Why do I feel like I did the wrong thing? It's like, no matter what I do, you're still here, even when you're not. Alive or dead, you're still hurting people. I wish I could just find a way to move on and forget about you.

I want a way to live my life without you being the center of it. Sometimes, I even dream about you and wake up crying. I'll figure out how to get past this. If you could just let me go.

Oh, and that funeral, are you kidding me? Those people in there would have died if they knew the real you and what you were capable of. All the crying and the flowers and sweet poems read for a woman who didn't care about her family enough to stick to just one. They would have walked out if they knew all about it. And you would have deserved it. You would have deserved worse. Maybe someday soon, everyone will know. I'd be happy to be the one to tell them, too. I had to stop myself from jumping up and telling everyone who you really were, what you were capable of. I could have told them everything you tried to keep hidden—all your dirty little secrets.

But there is something else, something you never knew about, something you never even suspected. But I know. And I've got a secret, just like you. Someone who was important to you but who's going to forget about you soon. All because of me. They deserve better than what you've done to them. They're the only person who makes me feel good now. And I'm going to give them everything you couldn't, everything you wouldn't. I'm going to make them love me. You'll be nothing but a distant memory to them soon, just a blip. A nothing. You'll be forgotten, and I'll still be here. And if anyone gets in my way, well, I know how to take care of that. You found out the hard way, didn't you? I did it once, and I'll do it again if I have to. It must be in my blood.

18

I'm lulled into a false sense of security when the next few days pass without incident. Katy doesn't skip school. In fact, her demeanor changes almost completely. She's pleasant to me again, if somewhat distant. I decided to not bother grounding her for the drinking incident. I don't think that would be much of a teaching moment anyhow. I let the monstrous hangover do that instead.

Amber continues to come over every evening. She offers to cook most of the time, and I have a hard time convincing her that I'm able to feed us adequately. Having someone around who's so worried about me and Katy is nice. Usually, we'll cook together or order takeout. Amber will stay until after dinner, sometimes later if we're watching a movie, and I can always look forward to a quick call or text from her in the mornings, too. She's becoming increasingly indispensable to me.

This morning, though, I'm alone in the house, alone in my studio. I'm just casually sketching. I don't have any particular commissions to work on at the moment, but I know that I'm going to have to network for jobs soon if I want to keep us fed.

We're okay for now, so I just use my time to sketch whatever comes to mind. I really liked the superhero sketches I did of Stella and Katy, so I've restarted the series since I tossed the originals in the trash. This time, they're just Katy. I'm in the middle of drawing Katy taking out a bad guy with her skateboard when my phone buzzes in my pocket. Distracted, I dig it out and answer without looking at the caller ID.

"Hello, Peter?" a man asks from the other end.

"Yeah," I say, my eyes still on the sketch. "Who's this?"

"It's Andrew."

I drop my charcoal pencil and watch it roll underneath the bookshelves where I keep my paints. "Dammit."

"Sorry. Didn't realize I'd get that sort of reaction." Andrew immediately sounds on edge.

"No, it's not you. I just dropped something."

But truthfully, it is partly about Andrew. I've put off contacting him because I just didn't want to. I'm trying to live in the moment, be here for Katy, and move past everything that's happened. Andrew is just a reminder of a time I'd rather forget. But it appears he's decided we need to hash this out.

"I'll be quick. We have some things we need to discuss," he says.

I hear shuffling paper and imagine Andrew in the office of his bookstore, shelves and opened boxes of books surrounding him. "You're right, we do. Why don't we set up an appointment with Stella's attorney? Go ahead and get all this business settled and behind us." I squeeze the phone between my shoulder and chin and squat down to fish around for my pencil.

"How about we meet before then? There are a few things I'd like to talk about before we involve the attorney."

"Uh, sure, yeah. I guess we can do that." My fingers close

over the pencil, and I retrieve it, smudging charcoal all over my fingers. I swipe them on the hem of my shirt.

"I'm free right now if you are." An urgency in Andrew's voice disturbs me.

"I'm busy at the moment," I reply, staring down at the sketch of Katy.

"We really need to talk," he repeats.

"Uh, okay. Yeah, sure." I don't feel like meeting with him, but I can tell he's not going to give up on this. I'd prefer to let the attorney take care of everything, but with him being so insistent, I know this is the only way I'm going to get rid of him. "What were you thinking?"

"There's a coffee shop on Main and Third. Uh, Good Beans or something."

"Cool Beans. Yeah, I know the place." *Strange that he seems to know this town so well.*

"What do you say to meeting there in an hour?" His voice becomes muffled as though he's placed his hand over the receiver to talk to someone. I glance at my watch.

"That could work for me. I can't stay long, though—I have to get Katy from school." I dust my hand off on my jeans, flip over the sketch of superhero Katy, and walk out of my studio, flipping the lights off behind me.

"Great. I'll see you there." He hangs up without saying goodbye.

* * *

I show up to the coffee shop ten minutes early. Something in me doesn't want to give Andrew the advantage of being the first one here. I want to be able to pick a table and order before he gets here, to establish a bit of a pecking order. A barista with a pierced nose, who looks roughly Katy's age, takes my order and tells me she'll bring it out to my table. I pick a table in the corner and put my back to the wall, facing the door. By the time Andrew walks in, I'm settled at the table with a cup of steaming coffee and a paper. He's five minutes early, and when he sees me already here, a look of annoyance flashes across his face. But he just gives me a nod and goes to make an order. He comes to the table a few minutes later with a cup of coffee and a pastry in his hand.

"Hope you don't mind. I haven't had the chance to grab lunch," he says, indicating the pastry.

"Not at all." I fold the paper, set it aside, and take a gulp of my coffee. "So what's so important you came all the way over to my town to talk to me?" As his nostrils flare, I suppress a smile, pleased to have gotten under his skin. Petty, but I can't help myself.

"I just thought we should talk. We didn't get the chance to after the funeral," he says.

"It was a busy day." I cross an ankle over the opposite knee and lean back. "So what do you need to talk to me about?"

"You know," he starts but pauses for a few seconds, probably gathering his thoughts or his courage or something. "Every time I see you, I wonder why Stella did it. We're so different."

I compare his broad shoulders and dark hair to my own blond lankiness and shrug. "She had varied tastes."

"I just can't believe she cheated on me with you." He snorts and shakes his head disbelievingly.

"Yeah, that's not quite what happened, pal. You weren't the one being cheated on. I was." I drop my leg and lean forward. "I came along first, remember."

Andrew's face reddens, and a muscle in his jaw tics. *Good. Get angry.* He's angry at the wrong person.

"Yeah, I remember," he says. "And just so you know, Stella and I were never legally married. She didn't seem overly worried about having a piece of paper to validate our relationship. She was a lot of things, but she wasn't actually a bigamist."

"Huh, thanks for that bit of information. Good to know." I can't keep the sarcasm from creeping into my voice. I don't ask him any more details about it because I really don't want to know, but he's probably just given me a legal out by running his mouth.

"Anyhow, I didn't come to talk about Stella." He puts down the pastry he's been holding and pushes it away. "It's Theo. He's being... difficult."

I sigh. "What does that have to do with me?" The last thing I need is Andrew confiding in me like we're friends and asking for advice. But on the other hand, if Theo is my son, then maybe I should hear him out and find out more about the boy.

"Theo and Katy are in contact with each other," Andrew says, flooring me.

"What?" I say. "That's not... She would have said something to me."

Andrew shrugs. "I hate to break it to you, but I've seen Theo's phone. I've seen their messages." It sounds almost like Andrew is warning me of something.

"So? Kids text. It's what they do. They're probably curious about each other. Seeing as they're brother and sister."

"Yeah, but... This is different." Andrew's voice lowers, and he checks the space around him.

"Different how? What kind of messages?" Nervousness starts to gnaw at my gut. I don't know if I can handle what I think he's about to say.

"They were very... flirtatious." Andrew quickly looks around. "Much too flirtatious to be brother and sister."

I explode. "That's fucking ridiculous!"

The barista glances over at us and clears her throat.

"Don't be stupid," I hiss more quietly.

"I'm not. I've seen the messages." His eyelid twitches.

"Why would you say some shit like that about my Katy?" I demand. "You're just being vindictive because you can't stand the thought of Stella being with me."

"That's not about this," he says through his teeth. "And has it escaped you that I'm also talking about my Theo? I'm not saying he's innocent in all this. I just thought you should know. Our kids are much closer than either of us realizes. Like, on-the-verge-of-a-relationship close."

I drop my arms and study Andrew. Nothing about him says he's lying. But I don't like the implication that Katy would consider something like a relationship with a blood relative. "I think you're reading too much into it. They're just a couple of kids. And Katy would never—"

"Yeah, well, Theo can be very persuasive. He's like his mom that way," Andrew says with a snort.

"About that," I say before I can stop myself, "are you even sure that Theo is yours?"

A sharp silence stretches between us after the words leave my mouth. That wasn't something I was ready to address, but Andrew pushed me too far. And I haven't been able to forget the thought that Theo might be my son. It's not beyond the realm of possibility. Having told Andrew as much, I watch as his face goes purple and a vein throbs in his neck.

"Watch your fucking mouth," he spits at me.

"You don't get to talk to me like that," I spit back. "Just because you happened to be fucking Stella doesn't mean shit. You said it yourself: you guys weren't even legally married.

I'm her legal husband, not you. I was here first, not you. And I just might be Theo's father. Not. You."

"You don't know what you're doing, man," Andrew tells me, his voice rough and shaking with anger. "You better rethink what you're saying to me."

"Or what? You gonna beat me up?" I laugh at him. "Go ahead. I don't care. After the beating I've gotten from Stella, nothing fazes me anymore."

He clenches his fists and obviously considers coming over to the table and pummeling the shit out of me.

I shrug at him. "Do your best."

"You leave Theo out of this." He glowers.

"You brought Theo into this. And my daughter. But know this: if you mess with me or Katy, I will get an attorney, I will get a DNA test done, and if Theo is my son, I will sue for custody. And I will win." I point at him with a tight grin.

Andrew shakes his head. "Well if we're not going to be adults about this situation, bring it on. Whatever any test says, Theo is my son and always will be. And he'd be better off with me considering how your daughter turned out."

My hands ball into fists. "Talk about my daughter one more—"

"Oh, save it, tough guy." Andrew stands, a cunning smirk spreading across his face. "I'm not afraid of you. You're nothing. You're the guy Stella fucked over because you're weak. Me? Well, I was distracted, I'm not gonna lie. But you. Mr. Stay-at-home dad, you should have noticed her lies. You were just too stupid." He laughs. "See you around, Peter."

As he walks out, I shove the table back an inch, rattling the coffee cups. A searing rage spreads through my limbs. I hate him. I actually hate him with every ion of my being.

19

I tap on the doorframe of Katy's room before cracking the door open and sticking my head in. I'm trying to give her some space, some privacy, but I have to talk to her about Theo before their relationship grows more complicated. If what Andrew said is true, anyway.

"Katy, can you come downstairs? I'd like to talk to you."

Katy is propped against the headboard of her bed, her phone in her hand. She glances up from the screen and sighs. "Yeah, I'll be right there." Then she turns back to her phone and smiles before clicking the screen off and heaving herself off the bed. "After you," she says with a gesture.

In the kitchen, Katy drops into a chair at the breakfast table and immediately tabs open her phone. I know kids are into their phones these days, but it's becoming an obsession with her now. And as much as I want to know what her and Theo's text messages say, I want to give her the privacy I think a seventeen-year-old girl deserves. So I refrain from asking her for her phone.

"You want some tea, honey?" I fill up the kettle and bustle around the kitchen. I figure it might be easier for Katy to talk to me if I'm not confronting her in some kind of interrogation —just a casual conversation. "Some toast maybe?"

"Uh, no thanks, I'm good." Her eyes are still on her phone, her fingers tapping at warp speed across the screen.

"I think I'm going to have some," I say.

She doesn't respond, buried in her phone again. I give up on the tea and grab a beer from the fridge instead. I pop the cap off and bring it to the table, where I sit down next to Katy.

"Hey, Katybug, let's talk." I sip the beer and try to look calm. "Can you put the phone down?"

"Yeah, sure." She sets the phone aside and gives me a fake smile. "That okay?"

"Uh huh. Listen, I'll just get right to it. I spoke to Theo's father, and he says you and Theo have been in contact with each other." I tap on the side of my beer bottle with my wedding ring. The clinking sound reminds me that I should take it off soon—no sense in wearing it any longer.

"I mean, yeah. I've been talking to Theo. So?" Katy's eyes slide to her phone.

I have to stop myself from reaching over and snatching it when it dings with a text alert.

"I don't know how comfortable I am with that," I say. "And I think he's... troubled."

"Troubled isn't the same thing as trouble, Dad. And he's not, really. He's just misunderstood." Her eyes slide back to her phone. "He's been through a lot."

Great. She's only seventeen and has already got a guy convincing her that he's not bad—it's just that no one understands him. Such a classic bullshit line. And it's even worse that it's Theo. I know that if I try to explain that "I'm misunderstood" is a classic guy tactic, she won't believe me.

"You've been through a lot, too. Do you think you're misunderstood?" I ask.

"I'm not the same as Theo. His dad is…" She stops and turns her head away. "I don't want to talk about it. It's private."

"Okay, we don't have to talk about it, then. But, Katy, are you guys just texting?" I have to tread carefully. I don't want her to think I'm accusing her of anything.

"Well, we've met up a few times," she confesses, her cheeks turning pink. "We just hang out."

"I'm not even going to ask if he's the one who supplied the vodka because, honestly, I don't think I want to know." I cool my hand off on my beer bottle and rub it along the back of my neck, which is rapidly heating up.

"I wouldn't tell you anyhow," Katy says stubbornly, giving me my answer. Of course it was him. "Is this all you wanted to know, if Theo and I are hanging out?" She reaches and grabs her phone, glancing at the screen.

"Mostly. And uh, you know, watch yourself. Theo is… going through some things, like you said. And he's younger than you. And he's your brother," I add like an afterthought.

Katy gives me a strange look. "Yeah, I know all that. Okay, I'm going to get my stuff for Kylie's sleepover tonight. "I'm not driving my car. I'll just walk over."

"I'll drive you," I say.

"Not necessary. I could use the exercise." She walks away.

I immediately think of everything I wanted to say to her but didn't—how much I wanted to warn her about Theo and how much I wanted to tell her to keep away from him but I didn't. Because telling her that would just drive them closer together. And one thing I don't want right now is Katy and Theo growing even closer.

* * *

I watch from the end of the driveway as Katy waves goodbye and starts down the street toward Kylie's house. I resist the urge to keep watching as she walks, like I did when she and Kylie were ten and would walk back and forth between our houses. Instead, I go back inside and decide another beer is in order. I pull one from the fridge, take it into the family room, and turn on the TV. I sit and scroll the channels, trying to find something worth watching. But all I can think about is Katy.

In the kitchen, on the side of the refrigerator, is a list of phone numbers, Katy's friends' parents. It's been there for years, updated when needed, a couple of names scratched out for the ones Katy is no longer friends with. And right at the top is Kylie's mom, Brenda.

I'm halfway through dialing her number before I even realize what I'm doing. *Am I really doing this—calling to check up on Katy?* I know Brenda won't mind, but Katy sure would. She would be furious with me if she thought I checked on her because I didn't believe she was there, that I thought she was out somewhere with Theo instead.

I even think about calling Andrew to see if Katy is over at their house. *He would tell me, right?* I know I said some pretty nasty things to him, but he's a parent. Surely, he would tell me if Katy was there. I put my phone down before I pick it back up and call Amber.

She answers immediately, and I hear the smile in her voice. I think of all the times I would call Stella when she was "working," and she wouldn't answer, or she would answer but would try her best to get me off the call quickly. It's nice to have someone answer who is glad to hear from me.

"Listen, I don't know what to do about Katy," I say to Amber. I tell her everything that happened with Andrew and what he said about Theo and Katy's texts. I tell her how I suspect Theo was the one who got Katy drunk. And I even tell her that I think Katy might be with Theo right now.

"I know what you need," Amber tells me.

"What's that?"

"You need to get out of the house. Let's get a drink."

I don't even have to think about it before I answer. "Yeah, that sounds great right now, actually. Sure, let's go get a drink. Let's get three."

Amber laughs and gives me the name of a small lounge nearby. I agree to meet her at her place in thirty minutes. Suddenly in a better mood, I run upstairs and change my shirt, brush my hair, and make sure I don't smell like a bear's armpit. And as I grab my keys and jump in the car, it occurs to me that I haven't felt this way in a long time. In a way, it almost feels like a date. The thought makes me smile, and I drive faster than I should on the way to Amber's.

20

"Just up here, on the right. It looks like there's street parking." Amber points toward a small storefront tucked away in a strip of other stores along Main Street.

I pull the car into a spot and kill the ignition. Before Amber opens her door, I jump out and run around to her side, pulling open the passenger door and offering her my hand. Then I feel like an idiot. I'm being ridiculous right now, treating this like some kind of date. Amber's just a family friend, and I'm definitely not over Stella yet. But I still open the bar door for Amber when we enter. I'm not rude.

She leads me inside, and we choose a U-shaped booth in the far corner. The bar is only slightly over half full, with a good mix of young hipsters playing darts and some office workers with their ties askew and jackets off, getting ready to sing karaoke. Red pendant lights hang over each booth, casting a warm glow over the tables. Amber slides into the booth, and I go to order drinks. The bartender, a young, bubbly blonde girl, gives me a toothy grin as she pushes my beer and Amber's wine across the counter to me. I slip her a good tip and gather up our drinks.

"So," Amber says after she takes a healthy sip of her white wine, "you're worried about Katy. And Theo."

"I am, yes. I just don't want the two of them getting too close." I feel uncomfortable even saying it, feeling like I've accused Katy of something.

"Listen, you have to go with your gut on this. Katy is a good kid. She's just going through a hard time. All this acting out? It's just her trying to sort through these really big emotions she's having." She pats my hand.

"I know, I know. But watching it unfold is killing me. And I don't think I'm helping matters one little bit." I sigh. "She's always been good. The perfect kid. Never in trouble at school. Never in with the wrong crowd and now... I'm just... I feel lost, dammit. Stella's death has really messed Katy up, I think. And what Stella's done has me questioning my entire life. Questioning whether I can trust myself. I mean, shouldn't I have picked up that something was off?" I pick at the label on my beer bottle. "It's messing with my head."

Amber appears to think carefully about her answer, but all she says is, "I can see how it would do that."

"I'm not sure what it's going to take for me to finally get over the shit Stella pulled." I down the rest of my beer in two gulps. "You need another?" I point at Amber's half-empty glass.

"No, thanks." She smiles, but it's forced and awkward. I see her eyeing my drink.

But I don't care. I need to numb the chaos under my skin. I make quick work of getting another drink, this time with a shot of bourbon on the side. Amber raises her eyebrows but doesn't say anything as I down the shot and chase it with my beer.

"So, Stella..." I lean back in the booth and drape my arms across the back.

"I thought you wanted to talk about Katy," Amber reminds me.

"I did. I do. But I feel like I can understand what Katy is going through better if I can figure out a way to explain to her why Stella was the way she was—why she felt like it was okay for her to play with so many people's lives. She betrayed us all, you know, not just me. Even you."

"I guess, yeah, in a way she did. Betray me, I mean," Amber says very slowly. She seems to not want to say anything bad about Stella, like she's trying to safeguard her legacy.

"You don't have to do that, you know. Be the diplomat." My words slur, but that doesn't stop me from going to the bar for another shot. I come back with another glass of wine for Amber, too.

"What do you mean?" Amber asks, picking back up on our conversation.

"You're avoiding saying anything bad about Stella," I say. "Like you want to protect her."

"No, that's not it," Amber says. "If anything, I'm trying to protect you and Katy."

"Oh, we'll be fine," I say, full of the bravado of a good bourbon. "I just want to know... You knew Stella in a different way than I did. How was she as a friend?"

Amber stares into her wine for a few heartbeats. "She was... guarded. Don't get me wrong. She was fun to be around—smart, you know. She was a good mentor, too. But she always seemed like she was holding back. I guess she was, though."

"Yeah, secrets." The "S" sound hissed from my mouth, and I'm aware I've had too much. But I still take a pull of my beer. "Or lies, whatever you want to call them." I look around, seeing if anyone is listening to our conversation before I move closer to Amber and bend my head toward her. "You think somebody did it?"

"Did what?" Amber asks, her eyes curious.

"Killed Stella, tossed her off that cliff?" The liquor makes my tongue bold. "Don't tell me you haven't thought about it."

Amber doesn't say anything, so I continue my drunken thoughts. "She lied—so much and to so many people. It's not beyond the realm of possibility that she pissed someone off enough that they just..." I mime pushing a person with my hands.

Amber glances around quickly. "Come on, now. That's just the beer. You don't really think that, do you?"

"It's just as plausible as an experienced hiker falling off a cliff in a spot she's hiked a hundred times." I shrug.

"Well, I'm going with the coroner's office on this one. She had an accident, Peter. And yes, she did some bad things, but she's gone now. But it's over. It's time for us to pick up the pieces she left behind and move on. And maybe put those pieces in the trash where they belong." Amber gives me a small smile.

"You're right. Of course you're right. I always knew you were a smart girl. Had to be, for Stella to like you." I'm rambling now, the drinks fuzzing my head pleasantly, making me almost forget why I ended up here with Amber in the first place. "You know, you've been so great, helping me. Helping Katy."

"Stop. I'm doing what any friend would do," she protests. But her cheeks turn a flattering shade of pink, and she looks pleased.

"I'm serious. You've been a rock... for both of us." I push my bottle away as the world suddenly sways. "I don't know what I'd have done without you."

Suddenly, Amber kisses me.

It's so sudden that, for a moment, I just sit there, letting her lips rest against mine, tasting the tart tang of her white wine. Then I pull back quickly because—*Stella. I can't do this to Stella. Amber is her best friend.* Then I remember what Stella did to us. So I take Amber's chin gently between my thumb and forefinger and kiss her back.

21

I pull away from Amber, slightly dazed. I can't believe that just happened. It never should have happened. *What kind of person am I, kissing my dead wife's best friend so soon after her death?* I'd like to blame it on the alcohol, but the truth is my attraction to Amber has grown over the past few weeks. Anybody would be attracted to her. She's pretty, smart, kind—much kinder than Stella ever was. But attraction doesn't excuse what I just did.

I get up from the booth, stumbling a bit as I struggle against the effects of the beer and bourbon. I fumble for my wallet and come up with a bill to put on the table. "Here, have another drink. I've really got to get home."

As I walk away, Amber calls out, "Peter, wait. It's okay. We didn't do anything wrong."

Hearing a threat of tears in her voice, I just keep walking without turning around. If I turn around, I'm going to be lost. I push through the door of the bar and stumble out into the night air. The street is quiet around me, my harsh breathing the only sound. I dig my keys out of my pocket and weave my way across the sidewalk to my car.

Only when I miss the unlock button on my key fob for the third time do I realize, somewhere in my beer-soaked brain, that I shouldn't drive. My car will be fine. I can Uber back to get it in the morning. But I don't want to wait for a ride now, so I take off walking, my footsteps echoing off the concrete. The street is empty, no cars passing me as I walk, so I look at my watch and realize the time is well after midnight. With a sigh, I realize I have a long walk ahead, so I shove my hands into my pockets and keep going.

Walking alone that late at night, though, when the world is so quiet, gives me too much time to think. And all I can think about is that I kissed Amber. And I know it's real because I still taste her lip gloss on my own lips. I run the back of my hand over my mouth, guiltily trying to erase the remnants of our kiss. I try to push everything out of my head and just concentrate on getting home. At least the cool air helps to clear my head.

When I'm halfway home, my phone pings, and I dig it out to find a text from Amber. She wants to know if I'm okay. I don't answer, not wanting to get into another conversation with her right now.

I do feel bad about just leaving her, though. Being drunk is no reason for me to be rude to her. She'll be okay, though, I think. She can have the bartender find her a cab or Uber home. Amber is definitely a big girl who can take care of herself. Hell, she's taken care of me for weeks now. *And I pay her back by leading her on. I'm an ass.*

After what feels like hours of walking, I finally make it home. I miss the keyhole twice before I'm finally able to unlock the door. I stumble inside, kicking my shoes off by the door, and snake my way down the hall toward the kitchen. Despite the late hour, coffee seems like a good idea right now. I need something to clear my head.

After a few tries, I finally get the coffee maker filled with water and grounds scooped into the filter, a good bit of them scattering across the counter in my attempt, which I just shrug off. *I'll clean the mess up later. And maybe right now, I'll just sit on the sofa and wait for my coffee.* I'm very tired, and the walk was long.

The pounding in my head beats over and over, making it ache. I screw my eyes shut tight, roll over, and hope the pounding will stop soon. After a few minutes, I realize my head isn't pounding—it's someone at my front door.

I open my eyes a slit, wincing as the morning sun feels like it's searing into my retinas. I'm in way worse shape than I thought I would be. The smell of slightly burned coffee makes me nauseated. My tongue is dry and stuck to the roof of my mouth, and I know my breath probably smells like bourbon-soaked shit. And I still hear that pounding. I should probably take care of it. I've got to do something to make it stop. Groaning, I push myself up off the sofa, holding my head in my hands.

I've lost a shoe, so I shuck the other one off and leave it beside the sofa. The banging still continues, so I yell down the hall, "I'm coming!" as I make my way slowly to the front door. Two figures stand beyond the frosted glass. A quick glance at my clock lets me know it's just past six in the morning. *Who in the hell is banging on my door so early?*

Oh my God. Katy. Something's happened to Katy. That thought spurs my movements, and I hurry toward the door, my head rapidly clearing. Something's happened to Katy while I was off kissing my dead wife's best friend and passing out from too much bourbon. I reach the door and fling it open.

And sure enough, two uniformed police officers are standing on the other side.

22

"Mr. McConnell?"

I blink rapidly against the light, squinting at the officers. A beefy man, the arms of his uniform shirt tight around his biceps, narrows his eyes at me and repeats my name. A shorter, trim blonde woman stands behind him.

"Uh, yeah, I'm Peter... McConnell. Is there something wrong?" I resist the urge to rub my eyes, instead blinking them rapidly to try to clear my vision.

"My name is Officer Sterling and this is Officer Quinn. You mind if we come in?" he asks.

I step back without saying anything and motion them inside. I glance quickly at the street and see their patrol car parked there. It's déjà vu, a repeat of the day Stella died. My heart thumps hard, and my head swims. I hurry past the officers, who slowly walk toward the rear of the house, their eyes roaming over everything.

Sterling stops in the door to the family room and sniffs the air. "You burn something?"

"Uh, no. Yes. Just some coffee I forgot about. Officers? What's going on? My daughter..."

"This isn't about your daughter," Quinn says.

Relief floods through my veins.

Quinn eyes my one shoe in the middle of the floor. The officers don't answer my question but instead follow up with one of their own.

"Where were you last night, Mr. McConnell?" Quinn asks. "Specifically between the hours of twelve and two in the morning?"

They both stare at me coolly. Sterling crosses his arms over his chest, making his shirt pull even more against his muscles.

"Uh, I was walking home," I say, embarrassment coloring my face. "I'm afraid I had too much to drink. My wife just died and... Well, it's been a stressful time."

"Was there someone with you?" Sterling asks.

"No, I'm afraid not. I was on my own. I left my car at the bar. I can give you the name." A throbbing emanates from my temples across my skull. I don't know whether it's from fear or the beginnings of a killer hangover headache.

"That's not necessary right now. What did you do after you walked home?" Quinn asks.

"Well, tried to make some coffee. And then I fell asleep on the couch, it looks like. And burned the coffee." I indicate the couch with its cushions in disarray and a blanket tossed over one of the arms.

"It looks like. So you don't remember?" Sterling asks.

The officers exchange a glance.

"Like I said, I drank too much. Look, what's this about?" Their glances make me nervous, and I shift back and forth on the balls of my feet.

"We'd like you to come down to the station and give us a

statement. Maybe answer a few questions for us," Quinn tells me. Her eyes continue sweeping the room.

"I'm not going anywhere until you tell me what's going on! And I need to call my daughter and make sure she's safe since you're not telling me anything," I say.

I search my pockets for my phone, frowning when I can't locate it. It must've fallen out and gotten lodged somewhere in the sofa cushions. I stalk over to the couch and pull the cushions aside.

"I'm sorry, Mr. McConnell. I'm going to have to ask you to come with us." Sterling places a firm hand on my elbow and tugs me upright.

"You're going to have to knock me out, then. I'm not going anywhere till I find out where Katy is."

I snatch my arm away, noting the look of rage that crosses the officer's face. He just might knock me out.

"He's right, Mr. McConnell. You need to come with us." Quinn gives Sterling a look. "You're wanted for questioning in connection with a murder."

My knees go weak, and I almost drop to the floor when what she said registers. *Murder?*

"You know a man named Andrew Ritchie?" Sterling asks, taking my elbow again, this time more roughly than before.

Confusion makes me stutter. "Uh, ye-yeah, I know him."

"Andrew Ritchie was murdered last night," Quinn says.

I take a step back in surprise. "Murdered? Are you sure?"

Quinn nods.

This is bad. So bad. I don't even have to ask. The police think I murdered Andrew Ritchie. My mind spins back to the night before. I walked home. I didn't go anywhere else. If I could find my phone, I could see when the last text came in from Amber. But I don't know what good that would do. Depending on when Andrew was killed, I don't have an alibi for last night. I left the bar around twelve—I remember looking at my watch. I don't know what time I got home or how long I took to walk from the bar. And Katy was out, so she can't vouch for me either. I'm stuck in a tight spot, and by the look on the officers' faces, they know it.

Then I remember the argument. *Oh, God.* If they find out about the argument, I'm done. All they have to do is find out the last time I spoke to Andrew. I'm sure the barista at the coffee shop heard more than enough to interest the police. The more I think about it, the bleaker the outlook becomes. They're really going to think I killed him. I think for a few minutes, my elbow still grasped in Sterling's clutch.

"Okay, I'll come down. But I want to call my attorney first."

The officers exchange a glance.

Quinn nods. "Yeah, okay. You're not under arrest, just wanted for questioning. You can call your attorney when we get to the station."

"Can I put on my shoes?"

"If you can find both of them," she quips.

I pull my arm out of Sterling's grasp and make my way to the closet near the front door, both officers on my heels. I pull a pair of running shoes and a jacket out of the closet and put them on.

"Okay, let's go. And I can walk on my own," I tell Sterling when he goes to grab my arm again. He shrugs and waves me toward the door.

It opens before we get to it.

Katy stands there in the doorway, her backpack in her hands. Her eyes widen when she sees the police, and she starts to shake.

"Dad, what's going on?" Her voice is tremulous. "Is something wrong?"

"It's nothing, Katybug. Everything is going to be fine. These officers just need to ask me a few questions." I look her over, making sure she's okay. I can't shake the feeling that she wasn't at Kylie's last night, that she was with Theo instead. And now Andrew is dead. But I'm not going to tell Katy that right now.

"Why?" She sounds like she's going to cry. Her makeup is smudged, and her hair is messy. She looks tired. She's never come home from Kylie's looking like this before. My Katy is usually bright-eyed and ready to take on the day in the morning. This Katy looks like she slept rough the night before.

"It's just a few routine questions, is all."

The officer tugs on my arm, moving me forward. Katy steps to the side and lets us pass. The officers lead me down the steps, toward the patrol car parked on the street.

I call back over my shoulder, "Call Amber."

The officers put me in the car and climb in front. And as we take off down the street, Katy is still standing in the front doorway, looking scared and alone. And it breaks my heart that I can't be there with her.

23

The officers drive me to the station, talking quietly between themselves. I can't hear a word they're saying because their murmurs are so low, but every once in a while, Sterling glances back over his shoulder at me. After only ten minutes, we reach the station, and Officer Quinn pulls the car to the rear of the building. The car slides into a marked space, and in seconds, Sterling pulls me from the rear of the car. I would say "helping," but that's stretching the truth. I glance around the parking lot. It's full of patrol cars and other unmarked cars, but we can't be seen from the street. I guess that's one blessing. It's bad enough that my neighbors may have seen me being carted off in a police car, but at least the entire town won't see me being escorted into the police station.

The officers enter through the rear door and check their weapons in with another officer sitting behind a frosted glass window. They lead me down a hallway with worn, gray carpet and into a room with a scuffed wooden table and a couple of hard-backed chairs. A window on one side of the room is covered in one-way reflective tint, and I notice a camera placed discreetly in one corner, near the ceiling. A red light blinks on its side.

"Have a seat. Someone will be with you shortly," Sterling tells me.

"Wait—you said I could call my attorney," I say quickly, before they can leave the room.

"Right. Uh, okay, stay right here," he says.

Like I'm going to get up and stroll out of the police station.

He leaves and comes back with a portable landline phone.

"Can I get a phone book, maybe? I don't have my phone, where I have the number," I say.

Sterling barely refrains from rolling his eyes, but he leaves and comes back with the book. I look up the number for Stella's attorney, the only one I know, and call him. I have to leave a message with his receptionist, but she reassures me that she'll send him straight to the station when he returns to the office. And she tells me to not answer any questions until he gets to me. After I finish, I return the phone and the book and settle into the chair.

"Might be a long wait," Quinn says. "Do you feel like answering some questions before he gets here?"

"I'll wait," I reply. I don't want to incriminate myself. It's not like I have any experience with police interrogations.

"Okay, boss," Sterling says with a shrug.

They leave the room without offering me a drink or the chance to use the restroom, so I know what kind of interrogation I'm in for. I sit quietly, glancing at the window occasionally.

I don't know how much time has passed because the room has no clock and I don't have my phone or my watch. I must've taken it off at some point last night. Hours might have passed by the time the officers finally come into the room or maybe only minutes—I don't know. I wonder how long they've spent looking at me from behind the one-way window. *And what do they see? Is there something about me that says "killer" to them? Something in the way I sit or dress, maybe? Have they already made up their minds about me without ever questioning me?*

When the door opens, I'm surprised to see Detective Anderson standing there with another, younger detective. They step into the room and close the door behind themselves. The younger detective moves a couple of chairs around to the opposite side of the table and takes a seat in one.

"Mr. McConnell, I didn't think I'd be seeing you again so soon," Detective Anderson tells me. "This is Detective Connor. We're just here to ask you a few questions."

"I'm waiting on my attorney," I tell them. "I'd like him here before I answer any questions."

"Yeah, yeah, of course. Not a problem. We can wait," Detective Anderson says.

The younger detective jots something in a small notebook. He sees me watching, clicks his pen closed, shuts the notebook, and gives me a tight smile. I can tell he already thinks I did it. Detective Anderson jerks his head toward the door, and they both leave me waiting again.

After what seems like an almost unendurable eternity, the door to the room opens again, and David Sheffield, Stella's attorney, steps inside. The detectives are on his heels. I stand up and hold my hand out to David.

"Thanks for coming," I tell him, shaking his hand vigorously. At least now I'll feel like I have someone on my side.

"Not a problem. You thirsty?" He looks at the detectives and clicks his tongue. "Tut tut, gentlemen. Let's get my client a bottle of water. This is no way to treat someone who has volunteered his time to aid your investigation."

After flashing the attorney a withering look, Detective

Connor leaves the room and comes back with a room-
temperature bottle of water. I nod my thanks, crack the seal,
and take a small drink.

"Okay, gentlemen," David says, settling into the chair
next to mine, "let's keep this brief. This man has a grieving
daughter to get back to."

"We'll keep it as brief as possible," Detective Connor
finally says. His voice is surprisingly deep. "Let's get started."
He pulls a small voice recorder from his pocket, clicks it on,
and sets it on the table between us. "Questioning of Peter
McConnell in the death of Andrew Ritchie, Saturday, three
thirty-six p.m."

I've been here for over eight hours, waiting. And Katy's
been home alone all this time. I hope she was able to contact
Amber and is with her right now. I hate to think of Katy alone,
not knowing what's going on.

"We'll start simple," Detective Anderson begins. "Mr.
McConnell, where were you last night between midnight and
two a.m.?"

I look at David, who nods. "Walking home from a bar."

"Why were you walking?"

"I'd had too much to drink," I say. "My car is still there,
parked outside."

"Did anyone see you walking?" Detective Connor asks,
flicking open his pen again.

"Well, Amber Sears. I was there with her," I tell them.

I keep looking at David, who's taking notes as well. But he
hasn't stopped me from answering any questions yet.

"Did she see you walking all the way home, or did she just
see you leave?" Detective Connor asks.

"You don't have to answer that," David tells me.

I nod and press my lips together.

"That's fine. We can ask Ms. Sears when we question her," Detective Connor says.

"Why would you question her?" I blurt. "She doesn't have anything to do with this."

"Shh, Peter. She's a potential alibi. It's okay," David reassures me.

I nod, my throat suddenly dry, and take another sip from the warm bottle of water. "Okay, okay." I nod again. "Go ahead. Wait. How did Andrew die?"

They ignore my question and follow up with more of their own.

"So your whereabouts are unaccounted for from midnight until the officers met you at your home this morning? Correct?" Detective Anderson asks.

David grabs my arm and shakes his head no before I can answer, so I keep my mouth shut.

"All right then, Mr. McConnell. You want to tell us about the last time you saw Andrew Ritchie?" Detective Connor asks this question without looking up from his notebook, and I know he already knows the answer. He just wants to see what I'm going to say.

"Sure," I reply with more bravado than I feel. "We met for coffee three, four days ago."

"And you had an argument with him there in the coffee shop?" Detective Connor pulls out a pair of reading glasses and slides them over his ears, which makes me wonder why he didn't do it before. He looks over the top of the glasses at me.

"You already know I did, so why are you asking me? David, how long do I have to stay here?" I ask.

I'm agitated, I've been here all day, Katy is alone, and the questions they're asking leave no doubt in my mind that they

think I did it. They think I killed Andrew. I can't help feeling like
if I don't get out of here now, then I never will. They'll fingerprint me, book me, and Katy standing on the porch watching me
led away by officers, confused and alone, is the last time I'll ever
see her. I stand up, but Detective Anderson is fast for someone
his age. He jumps up and puts a firm hand on my shoulder.

"I promise we'll be done soon. We're just trying to clear a
few things up," he says.

"Huh," I spit out, "looks to me like the only thing you're
doing is trying to pin a murder on me that I didn't commit."

"You know, you're the only person we've met with a
viable motive. Andrew Ritchie was a stand-up guy in his
town: business owner, donated to local charities, belonged to
the Chamber of Commerce, even served a term on the school
board." Detective Connor reads from his notebook. "You're...
an artist?" He raises his eyebrows at me.

"And that's a motive?" I ask, shaking my head with a wry
laugh.

"Nah, but him sleeping with your wife is. There have been
people murdered over a lot less," Detective Anderson says.
"You even threatened to take away his son."

How could they possibly know that? Theo, I realize. Andrew
must've told Theo, and Theo must've told the police this
morning. "Theo," I mutter. Then I remember that Andrew
was all Theo had. As far as I know, there's no more family.
Except maybe me. And Katy. "Where is he?"

"What?" David glances at me, his brows drawn low over
his eyes.

"Where's Theo at? His dad's gone now. He has no family.
Except Katy." I glance back and forth between the detectives.
"What? It's not like I'm going to go after him."

"All I can say is that he's in the custody of a foster family,"
Detective Anderson finally says.

"Is he okay? He wasn't... Did he find Andrew?" My heart constricts. I had no love for Andrew, but thinking about his son finding his body is almost too much.

"He's fine. He's safe, anyhow." Detective Connor says. He looks over at Detective Anderson as something passes between them. Detective Connor gives a brief nod and looks back at David. "Your client is free to go for now. Mr. McConnell"—he turns to me—"don't leave town."

"Okay, sure." I'm dazed, not sure what just happened. *Just like that?* It's over.

David pats my shoulder and thanks the detectives, and the next thing I know, I'm standing outside in the early evening light, next to David's red BMW.

"I'll take you home," he says.

Numbly, I nod, and get in the car.

"I can't believe this," I mumble, half to myself. "Poor Theo. First his mom and now his dad."

David shakes his head. "Poor kid. And how are you holding up?"

"I've been better but I'm muddling through."

"Look, Peter, just a word of advice. Ease up on the drink. You look, and smell pretty terrible and that's never great when the police are involved. Straighten yourself up."

Tears prick at my eyes. He's right. I know he is. I've made everything worse. Now I don't even have an alibi because I hit the self-destruct button and self-medicated with booze.

In less than ten minutes, I'm standing in the foyer of my home, Amber clinging to me and Katy watching me with narrowed eyes. Everything happened so quickly that my head is spinning. One minute, they were accusing me of murder, and the next they just let me go.

"Oh my God, Peter, are you okay?" Amber steps back and

studies me like she's looking for evidence the police beat a confession out of me.

"No, yeah. I'm fine, I'm fine." I turn to Katy. "Katybug, you all right?"

"Am I all right? No, of course I'm not all right!" Katy shouts at me, surprising me with her vehemence. Katy has never shouted at me before.

"I'm fine, honey," I say, thinking she's just worried about me.

"I can see that!" She's still shouting, but before I can ask her why, she storms up the stairs.

Amber and I both jump when her bedroom door slams so hard that it rattles the house.

"What was that?" Amber asks in a whisper.

"I don't know," I reply. Wearily, I pull off my shoes, kick them to one side of the foyer, and trudge to the kitchen. I haven't eaten all day, but I'm not hungry. I do pour myself a glass of cold water, though, and down it in a few gulps.

"Do you think she thinks I did it?" I point toward the ceiling with the glass in my hand.

"No, why would she think that?" Amber asks nervously. "Would you like me to make you a sandwich or something?" She tries to change the subject.

"No thanks," I tell her. "I don't know why she'd think that, but my best guess is Theo. Has she been on the phone a lot today?"

"Yeah. All day, pretty much, texting in between crying," Amber tells me.

I wince, thinking about Katy being home all day, not knowing what was going on.

"Yeah, Theo's gotten to her," I say. "Who knows what kind of ideas he's put in her head. That kid is... troubled."

"You're probably right," Amber tells me. "But you're home

now. I think you both need some sleep. And some food. I'll tell you what. You go take a shower, and I'll make some sandwiches for you and Katy and leave them in the fridge. I'll be gone before you're out."

"You don't have to do that," I tell her, but she's already moving toward the refrigerator.

"It's not a problem. I'm happy to help." She pulls out deli meat and mayonnaise.

"Okay, then. Thank you... for everything." I smile at her, happy to have someone who's on my side—someone I'm not paying to be on my side. "Oh, and Amber, about last night..."

"Don't worry about it," she says brightly, spreading mayo over slices of bread. "It's done, over with." She hums as she assembles the stack of sandwiches.

"Thank you," I say and turn to go upstairs.

When I finish my shower, I come back downstairs, hoping Amber is still around. But all I find is a stack of sandwiches in the fridge.

24

KATY

Softly, I crack open my bedroom door and peek around the edge. I listen for the sound of the TV or the Bluetooth speaker Dad sometimes uses in the kitchen. Nothing. He must be in his studio, sketching. Two days have passed since Andrew Ritchie was found dead, and I haven't seen Theo since. He texts me occasionally, but I think his foster parents might be strict about phone usage. I glance around once more and listen hard for the sound of footsteps. Then I close my door and lock it.

My room, even though it's on the second floor, is easy to escape. The window opens over the roof of the porch, and I can just step down from the windowsill to the gray shingles then quickly scoot over to the edge of the roof. Lattice wrapped with a climbing vine serves as my ladder, and I shimmy down quickly, glancing at the window of the living room as I jump the last couple of feet to the ground. I land on my knees and wince, but nothing is really hurt. I've done this half a dozen times already. I dust off my jeans, take one more look at the house, and sprint down the driveway, skirting the side with the decorative lighting, and take off down the street. Six blocks away, a dark-colored truck sits just outside the ring of light cast by the streetlights. I reach the passenger side, pull open the door, and climb in.

"Hey," Theo says with a smile, "I almost thought you weren't coming."

"I said I'd be here," I reply, "I mean what I say."

"It's okay. Don't be so defensive," he tells me. "Come here." When I slide over, he wraps his arms around me in a tight hug. "It's so good to see you." He lets me go and starts the truck, and we drive away down the street and out of the neighborhood.

"Whose truck?" I ask, sliding back into my seat and buckling the seat belt. I'm not sure I trust Theo's driving since he's only fifteen. "Do you even have a learner's permit?"

"It's my dad's. Was my dad's. Yeah, I have a permit." He glances over at me and gives me a mischievous grin. "You scared?"

"Maybe a little," I admit. I tighten my seat belt and watch through the window as he steers us through the streets. After a few turns, I realize where we're going. "Back to the mountain. You're obsessed with that hiking trail, I swear."

He doesn't answer me, just steers us into the parking area and parks the truck in the rear, where the security lights don't quite illuminate the corners of the lot. He puts the truck in park and cuts the engine, leaving us sitting in the dark. The faint moonlight is barely enough to make out the planes of his face. I hear his seat belt click, then he faces me. He takes my hand and holds it tightly.

"I've missed you," he says.

He rubs a thumb along my knuckles, and goosebumps erupt along my arms. I try to twist my hand away, but he tightens his grip.

"I... missed you, too. There's been so much going on." I can't stop the tears that suddenly flow.

"No, no, don't cry, Katy. Everything's going to be okay." He moves close, so close that I can almost feel his breath on my cheek.

"How do you know?" I sniffle. "What if we really messed up? Aren't you scared we'll get caught?"

"No," he says emphatically. "I can't think like that." He stops as a car pulls through the lot, its headlights piercing the darkness and highlighting his face for a moment. In the brief light, his face is dark and forbidding. "I've got too much to lose now." He flips my hand over and runs his thumb across my palm.

"I just... I'm so scared. And ashamed, too. I'm ashamed of what we've done. I'm not sure I can live with... what we've done. I feel like my mom, lying to everyone. I don't know how she did it." In the pale light, I watch his thumb sweeping back and forth across my hand. I want to pull it away, but I know it will make him angry.

"You're nothing like her," he says to me. "Nothing. Don't ever think that way. She did really bad things, but you... You're sweet and kind, nothing like her."

"I knew about her, you know," I tell him. "I knew she was having an affair." I sniff back the tears. "I knew what kind of person she was before she died, and I never told anyone."

"Let it go," he says. "She isn't worth your tears. She got what she deserved." He gives a shrug and lets go of my hand.

I rub at my palm, trying to remove the sensation of Theo's thumb from my skin.

"This was a mistake," Theo says. "I'll take you home."

"Not yet," I say. "It's so lonely there. And chances are Dad is just hanging out with Amber anyhow. She's always there."

"Really?" Theo asks, sounding interested. "Tell me more about that."

So we sit in the dark for a while, and I tell Theo about the way Amber's always been around since our mom died and how she helps Dad with the cooking and cleaning. And he just sits there, a small smile playing around his lips as he listens. That smile makes my stomach churn, like there's something not right about it. But I shrug it off and keep talking because I feel like I need Theo and Theo needs me. I'm all he has now, and I want to be here for him, no matter what.

25

I'm in the kitchen, getting a glass of water and contemplating making something for dinner, when a quiet knock startles me out of my thoughts. I place the glass down on the counter and find Amber standing at the kitchen door. She holds up a bag and waves through the window. I hurry over to let her in.

"Thanks," she says, putting the bag on the table. "I figured you hadn't had any dinner yet. And it looks like I'm right. It's getting kind of late. Here, burgers." She pushes the bag across the counter at me. "No onions for Katy—is that right?"

"Yeah, that's right." I snag the bag and open it.

As it crinkles under my fingers, the delicious smell of grilled beef wafts out.

"I didn't realize how hungry I was, actually. Thanks." I pull out a burger, the wrapper just slightly greasy, and open it. "Oh, but Katy probably won't bother to eat with us. She's still avoiding me."

"That's okay. We'll just leave it in the fridge, and she can warm it up in the middle of night and eat it in the corner like some kind of burger goblin." She rustles around in the bag and comes up with her own burger and container of fries. "Want to share with me?"

"Sure, but I take lots of ketchup," I warn her.

She just rolls her eyes before reaching into the bag and pulling out a handful of ketchup packets. "I remembered."

We sit at the breakfast table, and the only sound for a few minutes is us munching on our late-night dinner.

"So," Amber asks, swiping a dusting of salt off her fingers, "have you heard any more from the police?"

"Nuh uh," I mutter around a mouthful of burger. I swallow quickly. "I talked to David today, too, and he hasn't heard from them either. Do you think it's weird? If they were going to arrest me, wouldn't they have done so by now?"

"I'm not really sure how this works, Peter. I'm no expert on police procedure." She pushes away her unfinished burger and gets up to get a drink from the fridge. She comes back with a couple of beers, pops the top on both, and slides one across the table at me. "Have you heard anything about how Andrew—you know—what happened to him?"

"No, I've been avoiding the news. But I think I should probably find out." I push the fries away, my appetite gone.

Amber searches her pockets and comes up with her phone, giving me a quick glance before she starts tapping away. She reads something on the screen, and her mouth tightens into a thin line. She swipes away whatever was on the screen and reads something else. "Do you want to know?" she asks me.

"No. Wait." I sigh. "Yes, I need to know."

With a swift nod, she turns her phone around and I see an article, "Local Man Found Dead" on the screen. I take it from her hand, scroll down, and read the article.

"Blunt force trauma," I mutter, "no known suspects. Does

that mean they ruled me out?" I look at the date on the article, and my heart falls when I notice it was written only hours after Andrew was found. "Oh, the writer wouldn't have known about me then. So I might still be a suspect." I pass Amber's phone back to her and sit thinking about the article.

"He could have just hit his head? Right? Taken a fall or something." Amber scrolls through a couple more articles, chewing nervously on the inside of her cheek. I can't help but think how sweet she is to be so worried about me.

"I suppose so, but you know they never include all the details in these articles. The police omit stuff so they don't give away anything that could help them with solving the crime." I start cleaning up the leftovers from our dinner. "So they have something that makes them think it was a murder and something that makes them think it was me."

I turn away so that Amber won't see the worry on my face. She's been by my side through everything lately, and I don't want her to think I'm weak, that I can't handle everything myself.

"You know, there's something I've been thinking about," Amber says, sliding her phone back into her pocket. "Um, the kiss? I said don't worry about it—it's over, right? But I can't stop thinking about it."

An electric shock jolts up my spine. I let out a soft breath.

"I have, too," I confess.

"It's just that, if I'd never kissed you, you wouldn't be suspected of murder." Amber sniffles as tears gather in the corners of her eyes.

"What? No, wait. That's... that's not even remotely true, Amber. You can't blame any of this on a kiss."

This isn't the turn I expected this conversation to take.

"If I hadn't kissed you, you wouldn't have gotten upset and left." She rubs her nose with the back of her hand. "I could have been your alibi, and I messed it all up." The tears start in earnest this time, sliding silently over her cheeks. "It's my fault."

"Neither of us is at fault for that. We had a lot to drink, and things got, well, not out of hand, but... you know what I'm saying. It's not your fault. It's entirely mine, I shouldn't have drank so much. I was just stressed, worrying about Katy, and you tried to cheer me up. I can't have you blaming yourself for something that isn't your fault." I push aside the detritus from dinner and reach over to grab her hand. "It's not your fault," I repeat.

"Okay, but I could help you. I could go to the police, tell them I was mistaken about the time and that you were with me." She rubs her nose again, prompting me to hand her a napkin from the burger bag. She wipes her nose and crumples the napkin in her hand. "I can help."

"That's incredibly sweet of you," I say, touched by her desire to help, especially since doing so could get her in trouble as well. "I can't let you do that."

"Then what are we going to do?" She rubs her clenched hands across the tops of her legs, her voice shaking. "I don't want you to go to prison, Peter."

"I don't want that either," I say with a wry laugh. "But what I want you to do is not worry about me. Speaking of worrying about someone, did you get home okay that night? I'm sorry that I left you stranded."

Amber brings the napkin to her nose again and rubs. "Uh huh," she mutters through the thin paper material, but she doesn't tell me how she got home. I just assume she caught an Uber and don't push her anymore about that night. I don't want to make her cry again. I finish cleaning up the table and toss the trash into the wastebin.

"You know," I say, looking at the last burger, meant for

Katy, "Katy really should eat something. She hardly eats these days. If I leave this here, she'll probably ignore it, and then you've wasted your efforts to keep us fed. I'm going to go get her."

"I'll finish cleaning up." Amber gets up and grabs a dish towel to wipe the table, still sniffling.

Heading upstairs, I note how quiet it is. I wonder if Katy is asleep and debate with myself on bothering her. I don't want to wake her up if she's resting. But the kid has to eat, so I rap on the door with one knuckle and wait for a long stretch before knocking again. "Katy," I call through the door.

No answer.

I try the knob and find the door locked. Jiggling the handle, I call her again. Still no answer. The door is locked. She has to be in there. *Why isn't she answering me?* A thousand scenarios flash through my mind at warp speed, all of them ending with Katy hurt or worse. I picture her lying on her floor, her head covered in blood like Andrew's, like her mother's.

I jiggle the doorknob harder. "Katy Ann, answer me!"

Still no noise.

Stepping back, I ready myself to put my shoulder to the door and shove until it pops open. When I'm just about to rush the door, it pulls open a crack, and Katy peers out. "Dad?"

I stop myself from ramming into the door. "Why didn't you answer me?" I put a hand on the top of the door and push, but Katy leans into the door, preventing me from opening it fully.

"I... I was napping, and I had to put on some shorts," she answers. "Sorry." The word comes out long and drawn out and full of sarcasm. "Can't I get any privacy around here?"

"Oh, you get plenty of privacy around here. I never see you," I tell her, my hand still on the door.

Her only response is to roll her eyes and sigh heavily.

"Yeah, that's pretty much how I feel about everything these days, too. Anyhow, there's a burger downstairs with your name on it. Amber brought them by. I want you to come down and have something to eat. You're starting to waste away."

I move my hand, and Katy slams the door so hard it would've taken off my finger if I hadn't snatched it away.

"Come down and eat," I say through the door. I know I won't get an answer, so I just head back down the stairs. Halfway down, it occurs to me that, for someone who'd just been sleeping, Katy looked very red. And slightly sweaty.

I resist the urge to turn around and go back to Katy's door and demand she let me in. She would probably just lock me out again anyhow. But more is going on with her than just grieving for her mother—something I can't put my finger on. And I'm stung by the realization that Katy is almost an adult and all I can do is stand back and let her make her mistakes. I just hope she knows she can come to me if whatever trouble she's in is something she can't handle on her own. I hope she knows she's not alone.

26

Dear Mom,

Why is it that I'm constantly having to clean up your messes? Even when you're gone, I'm still coming in and sweeping up behind. Just like you to start a fire and then watch while everything burns down around everyone else. Typical, selfish Stella.

Don't you worry about it, though. I'm just tying up some loose ends, is all. My plan is beginning to come together perfectly. I'm sure you'd be proud of me. I might be turning out just like you, the ultimate manipulator. And now, there shouldn't be any more interference. Everything's going to be perfect.

27

The lobby is surprisingly luxurious, with a thick carpet and plush chairs in the waiting area. A petite blonde receptionist welcomes me when I walk in and offers me a water or juice. I take the water and pick a chair. The room is quiet, the lush furnishings muffling even the click of the receptionist's nails on her keyboard. I stare at the framed prints of beach scenes on the walls. I always wonder who decorates these places and doctors' offices too. *Is there some website somewhere that sells art prints specifically for attorney and medical office waiting rooms?* I swear they're all the same. I've shifted to flipping aimlessly through an architecture magazine, the homes and offices decorated much like the room I sit in now. I toss the magazine to one side, too agitated to concentrate on its glossy pages.

When I dropped Katy off at school, I didn't tell her where I was going or what I was going to try and do. If what I think is true and if I can do what needs to be done, our lives will change forever. Again.

"David's ready for you," the pretty receptionist says with

a smile. She gets up and opens a large wooden door and beckons me through.

After I step inside, she steps in behind to check with David and make sure everything is all right. Then she closes the door gently behind herself and leaves me facing Stella's lawyer, sitting behind his oversized mahogany desk.

"Peter, have a seat." He indicates the oxblood chairs facing his desk. I pick one and lower myself into the soft leather.

"Nice place," I say, looking around.

The artwork here is more masculine, hunting scenes and dark woods.

"I do try. Anyhow, what did you need to see me for? More trouble with the police? I figured you'd call if they wanted to question you again." David leans down and pulls a diet soda from beneath his desk somewhere, probably a mini fridge tucked away. "You want one?" He holds out the can.

"No, thanks." I tip my water bottle in his direction. "No, not the police—at least not directly. I'll get right to the point. Theo Ritchie."

"Andrew Ritchie's son? What about him?" David pulls over a legal pad and uncaps an expensive-looking pen.

"I don't think we know that he is, conclusively, Andrew Ritchie's son," I tell him. "There's a very strong possibility that he, well, that he could be mine." I lean forward and place my water bottle on the edge of his desk.

"Right, right." David temples his fingers under his chin. "What are you trying to ask me to do, Peter?"

"I want a DNA test. I want to prove conclusively who Theo's father is. Me... or Andrew. Can you help me?"

David stares at me for a moment, his fingers tapping against his chin before he finally, carefully tells me, "Yes, I can help you. And for Stella's sake, I will. Theo is her son, and he deserves to have a family. It won't be easy, though. Theo isn't old enough yet to consent to a DNA test, and he's a ward of the state now. There's going to be a lot of red tape to get through to make that happen." He reaches for his pen and scribbles notes on the pad. "It's all going to have to go through the courts. And family court isn't easy to deal with. But with enough time and money, we can make it happen."

Money. I think about my current situation, my lack of a real job. Being freelance doesn't really rake in the cash. But I'll do what I have to, refinancing the house or borrowing against the equity, whatever it takes to prove that my hunch is right, that Theo is mine.

I nod at David. "Yes, let's see if we can make it happen."

"Right." He takes a few more notes. "Are you sure this is what you want? What happens if he's not yours? If Andrew Ritchie really was his father?"

"Is it possible that I'd be able to become a foster parent, take him in that way? Katy is his sister, you know, the only family he has left. Well, that we know of, anyhow." I don't mention to David the suspicions Andrew voiced about Katy and Theo. Those seem so sordid. I'll keep that to myself for now. "Even if he's not mine, I still want to help him. I know he's a troubled kid, but... I feel like I should do something."

"That's very noble of you, Peter."

"Thank you. But I'm not doing it to be noble or trying to be a hero or something. The kid has just lost both parents. I don't want him to get stuck in the foster system. If I can help him, I will." The words sound so focused, but inside, I have to admit I'm a mess of conflicting emotions. I stare down at my lap to stop David from noticing them.

"There's just one thing. What makes you think Theo Ritchie will want to come live with you, whether you're his father or not? As far as he knows, you may have killed

Andrew, the only dad he's ever known." David's fingers tap quickly on his notepad as he studies me over the top of his glasses.

"I'm hoping he'll take into account the fact that I was questioned, not arrested. And maybe Katy can help me a little, you know, with persuading him. I think they're... friends. Now." I clear my throat and reach for my water.

"Well, okay then. I'll get paralegal started on drawing up some of the court documents we're going to need to file. I'll likely need some paperwork from you at some point. And you're going to have to come in and sign a few things. Well, probably a lot of things." He writes quickly while he talks. "I have a lab I use for custody cases. Someone will contact you about collecting DNA, probably in the next few days. That sound good?"

The speed at which everything is taking shape makes my head spin, but it's everything I wanted to hear. I have someone on my side, someone who can give me some real help. Expensive help, but real.

"Sounds great," I tell him.

"Okay, is there anything else I can help you with?" He's already half out of his chair, his hand extended, so I tell him no. "Good, good. Shelly, out in the lobby, will take your call anytime. You'll be hearing from me soon."

We finish up our goodbyes, and I head back out through the plush lobby, saying goodbye to pretty Shelly as I pass, and make my way outside with a heart slightly lighter than it's been in a while.

I've just pulled into the driveway when my phone buzzes. I search my pockets and pull it out, looking at the text that's popped up on my screen, from Amber.

Hey, how did your meeting go?

I ping off a quick response. *Fine. David was very helpful. It's a lot, though, so I'll tell you next time I see you.*

And are you okay? she replies.

I'm fine. Just got home.

How about I come over? I can cook you guys some pasta, she sends.

I love how she never leaves Katy out of the equation.

Maybe some other time. I have a lot to talk to Katy about, I send back.

Okay, sure! Just let me know when.

She ends her text with a series of smiley, winking emojis, which makes me laugh. Everything is coming together, I think. Now, I just have to work on Katy. I shove my phone back into my pocket and head inside.

"Katy," I call as soon as I open the door. "Katybug, come on downstairs."

I head into the kitchen, unload my pockets onto the counter, and grab a beer from the fridge. After poking around in the pantry to see what I can make for dinner, I grab a container of jarred sauce and some pasta, ready to make a quick dinner. I hope Katy and I can cook together, like we used to, and talk. If she would ever come down.

Exasperated, I leave everything on the counter and start to make my way upstairs, but a ding from my phone stops me. I turn around and grab it to look at the screen.

Hey Dad out with a friend don't wait up.

Great. I don't even bother texting to ask what friend because I'm pretty sure I already know. Retrieving my beer, pasta forgotten, I head into the family room and sink onto the couch, flipping on the TV. It's getting close to sunset and I can't help but think about Katy out there. Please let her be with Kylie, not Theo. I'm not sure I can cope with her sneaking away to see a kid who just lost both parents.

Theo might be vulnerable but so is Katy. While Theo has that angry teen boy aura to him, Katy is naïve and innocent.

Corruptible.

I push the thought out of my head and flick through channels as sip my beer. Suddenly, it's unbearable. It's not enough. I've spent plenty of nights alone on the sofa, watching TV, while Stella was out living her double life. But now, I'm tired of being alone. Maybe I was tired of it then, too, and just didn't realize, but now I do. I don't want to be alone right now. I want someone to talk to. And I know who.

I don't text or call. I just get in my car and drive the short distance to Amber's. She opens the door and greets me with a smile, happily ushering me into her home. I follow her down the short hall to her kitchen, watching her hips sway as she leads the way. And I'm suddenly pretty sure I made the right decision. Here is where I want to be.

28

Amber leads me back into the kitchen and, with a smile, tells me to park it on one of the barstools at the counter. She bustles around the kitchen in a pair of shorts and an old T-shirt from Stella's company. Her hair is pulled up into one of those messy buns all the girls seem to know how to do. I've always thought it was a kind of sexy look, but Stella always kept her hair in a sleek bob. More professional, she always said.

Amber busies herself making drinks and brings me one of the best-looking martinis I've ever seen. I take a sip, and it's so cold that it practically bites the inside of my cheek.

"Perfect." I take another sip.

Then she slides a plate of homemade cookies in front of me.

"Okay, now you're just spoiling me." I grab one of the cookies from the plate. "And they're still warm. Oh my God." I bite into one, and it practically melts away on my tongue. "I gotta tell you, Amber, this is pretty close to perfect."

"Well, thank you. I do try. What brings you by, anyhow?

How'd your talk with Katy go?" She slides onto the stool next to mine and reaches for one of the cookies.

"Um, well, I don't know. There wasn't any talk because Katy wasn't home. She texted and said she's out with a friend." I take another gulp of the ice-cold martini. "This really is fantastic." I tip the glass at her.

"So, tell me, how was your meeting? You said you were meeting with your attorney, but you didn't mention about what. Something to do with Andrew Ritchie?" She pops a piece of cookie into her mouth.

"Not exactly," I say, picking up my own cookie. I chew thoughtfully before finally swallowing. I decide to be as straight with Amber as I was with David. "I want to do a DNA test on Theo, to find out if he might be my son. And I want him to come live with us, with me and Katy, even if he's not. I can't leave the kid to rot in foster care."

"I don't know," Amber says carefully, trying to not say anything that will hurt my feelings. "You know, he might want to stay with his foster family. The Ritchies and the McConnells don't exactly have the best history together. Plus, what if Andrew Ritchie has relatives. He might want to live with them."

"That's true. And it's fine if he wants to stay with relatives. But I don't think he would've gone into foster care if he had family willing to take him in." I shake my head, freeing some of the worries from my mind. "Well, I at least want to give him the option, to let him know he's not alone." I finish my drink, and Amber immediately makes me another.

"Come on," she says, grabbing my drink and leading me into the living room. "It's more comfortable in here." She opens her phone and pulls up a playlist, and soon soft music is playing from a Bluetooth speaker somewhere in the room. She climbs onto the couch and tucks her legs underneath herself, patting the cushion next to her. "Wow, imagine if Theo does live with you. Wouldn't it be strange?"

I nod before sipping my drink. "Yes. At first. Especially with Katy..." I trail off, not wanting to complete that thought. I was going to say especially with Katy and Theo flirting with each other, but I stop myself in time.

The truth is, I'm terrified about the prospect of Theo and Katy getting too close. But that's because they haven't grown up together and they don't consider each other family. If I adopted Theo, Katy would be forced to see him as her brother.

At least that's the theory and one of my main motivations. I also don't want him to be left behind either. The kid has been through more than any fifteen-year-old should go through.

"Such a kind heart," Amber mumbles.

I pull back from my thoughts to see Amber gazing at me. Her expression is soft and sweet and a tingle runs through my limbs. It's been a while since anyone looked at me like that.

The next thing I know, her arms are wrapped around my neck, and she's in my lap. Her lips are on mine, and we sink into the sofa together. And for a moment, I think about pulling away, but she's so warm against me, and her lips are delicious with the flavors of chocolate and vodka. So I wind my fingers into her bun and tug it down as I press my lips into hers.

Amber's fingers fumble the buttons on my shirt. A small voice tells me to stop her, to set her aside gently and tell her no, but my body overrides my alcohol-soft brain, and when she pulls on my belt with a questioning look in her eyes, I just nod yes and kiss her again. Amber shifts and pulls me on top of her, and I close my eyes, and warmth washes over me as I push into her.

I'm lost in the moment when she whispers in my ear, "I've wanted this for so long."

I tip my head back in ecstasy, lost in her, letting all the worry and stress leave my body.

Afterward, I feel the need to apologize, but I don't know how to tell Amber that what just happened was a mistake. She's back in the kitchen in nothing but her T-shirt now, humming as she makes us another drink. I pull my pants back on and search for my shirt and find it crumpled and shoved halfway underneath a cushion. I try to brush the wrinkles out but give up eventually when they prove too stubborn. Scrubbing my hands across my face, I try to wipe away the fogginess of martinis and sex before I go back into the kitchen.

"Oh, no more for me, thanks," I tell Amber as she offers me another drink. "I've got the drive home."

"Oh, you're not leaving already, are you?" Amber's face falls, but before I can say anything, she smiles at me again. "It's okay—I'm not driving. I'll drink for both of us."

"I should... find my shoes," I say awkwardly, backing out of the kitchen and into the living room.

"Peter, do you want to talk about it?" Amber is standing in the doorway with a drink in her hand.

I flounder, not sure how to broach this. "Listen, Amber, it was great. You were great, but..."

"Go ahead and say whatever it is you want to say," Amber tells me.

She's so sweet, so pretty with her hair down and mussed by our lovemaking. I don't want to hurt her or make her angry, and I regret what just happened. It's too soon—Stella hasn't been gone long. And I don't know how it would look, me starting up something with Stella's best friend barely weeks after her funeral. I can't let Amber or Katy be subjected to the kind of rumors that would start swirling through the grapevine if we started seeing each other.

"Amber, I like you, I really do. You've been such a help to me recently and to Katy, too. You're smart and pretty and kind, really everything any man would look for in a woman..."

"But," she prompts me when I stop.

"Yes, there is a *but*, and it's me. I can't get into anything now, like a relationship. It's too soon, and I'm still raw, still healing from Stella and her betrayals. It wouldn't be fair to you, to ask you to deal with all my baggage when I'm not ready to deal with it myself. Then there's everything with Theo, you know, and the DNA test. Now is just not the time for us." I say everything quickly, my heart plummeting as I wait for her reaction.

She stands there for a few moments before downing her drink in one swift gulp. "I understand. I really do. I'm not going to say I regret tonight because that's far from the truth. And I'm willing to just be your friend, for now," she says with a quick smile. "I think you're worth waiting for, Peter. I'll be here when you're ready."

"Thank you," I say breathlessly. "You really are a remarkable woman." Clearing my throat, I glance around the floor. "Uh, you haven't seen my shoes, have you?"

She smiles, her eyes sparkling, and points at the coffee table. "I think they're under there."

"Ah, right. I should get going, so..."

"Of course you should. I know you have things to do. Let me get some of those cookies wrapped up for Katy, though. They're her favorite." She trots back into the kitchen, and I swear she puts extra sway into her hips. And when she glances back over her shoulder to see if I'm watching, I know she is. With a knowing giggle, she continues into the kitchen, and I bend over to look for my shoes.

Sitting on the couch, I reach under the table and pull out my shoes, glad that I somehow managed to stuff the socks inside. As I slip into my socks, I hear the ding of a cell phone message. At first, I think it's mine, but then I see Amber's phone on the edge of the table.

I don't even know what possesses me to lean over and look at it, but I do.

The name of the texter takes me by surprise. My heart thuds harder. Then I read the message and my blood runs cold.

Don't worry, I have Katy in the palm of my hand.

Sent from Theo.

29

The text alert disappears and, with it, the text itself. I throw a glance at the door to the kitchen. The sound of cabinet doors opening and closing tells me Amber is still moving around in there. Before I can change my mind, I tap the button on Amber's phone and try to open it.

It's locked with a passcode. *Dammit.*

Wondering what her passcode could be, I just try 1-2-3-4. It doesn't work. I can't remember her birthday. I think it's sometime in September, but I could be wrong about that, too. I have no reason to remember her birthday.

I can't let Amber walk in here and catch me with her phone in my hand. I'd never be able to explain something like that. She's still in the kitchen, but she won't be for much longer. My eyes dart around, searching for something, anything, to give me an idea of what her passcode might be, but it's fruitless. She's certainly not going to have it painted on the wall like a mural.

"Hey, Peter," Amber calls from the kitchen.

I freeze, phone still in my hand. "Yeah," I call back, but my voice is stuck in my throat. I clear it and try again. "Yeah?"

"I just wanted to make sure it's okay for me to come by tomorrow." Her voice grows closer. "Just a friendly visit. I'd like to check in with Katy, too. Maybe I could take her for ice cream."

Just before she appears in the doorway, I shove her phone into my back pocket. She's standing on the threshold, a lidded plastic container in her hands. I know my face is screaming, *"I stole your phone,"* right now. She can't miss the fear of being caught on my face. But she doesn't tell me to give her phone back or scream and demand to know what I'm doing. She just stands there, smiling at me with a container of cookies in her hands.

"Uh, yeah, I don't see why not. I'm sure Katy would like that." I don't know how to keep my voice from breaking. "I should really get going, though." I almost sprint across the room to her, I don't want her to look at the table and realize her phone is gone.

"Sure. Here you go." She holds out the container, and I stare at it like it's going to bite me before finally realizing that to look normal and not like a phone thief, I need to reach out and take it from her. So I do.

"Okay. See you tomorrow, then?" She still stands there, smiling at me.

I pray that her phone doesn't ding again with another alert, Theo texting to see why she hasn't answered, maybe.

"Not a problem. I mean, yeah. I'll tell Katy. Uh, tomorrow." I stumble over my words and almost over my feet as I back away from Amber.

I back all the way across the room, making her giggle. I hope she thinks that I'm just being an awkward-after-sex kind of guy and not a sneaky, thieving kind of guy. When I reach the hallway, I finally turn and hurry toward the front door, hoping to get out before Amber stops me again. Thievery is not my forte, it turns out.

I rip open the door and run, almost plunging through the box hedges surrounding her entryway in my haste to get out. I stumble over the pathway bricks and finally make it to my car. Fumbling with my keys, I get the door unlocked and jump into the driver's seat, tossing the cookie container over my shoulder into the back seat without looking, not caring if the cookies spill out. I back out of the driveway as quickly as I can, revving the engine too high, and take off down the street toward home. I can't help but think I'm going to look out my rear window and see Amber chasing my car, waving her fists and shouting accusations at me. But she's not there. The only thing I see in my rearview mirror is my own guilty face.

A few minutes later, I pull into my driveway and slam the car into park then jump out and run to the door like hell-hounds are on my heels. I snatch the door open, and once I'm in, I slam it behind myself. Leaning against the hallway wall, I try to slow my rapid breathing and fast-beating heart. This may be the closest I've ever come to thinking I might be having a heart attack.

Guilt overwhelms me. I can't believe I stole someone's phone. And not just any someone—Amber. It feels like a betrayal. I don't know how she's going to feel when she finds out, and she'll find out eventually. I just hope I can explain to her why I did it. I need to know why Theo is texting her and why he's texting about Katy. About having Katy under control.

I could've asked, but my instinct screams at me not to. If Theo is texting Amber about my daughter, then it isn't good. They're up to something and now I have to try to figure out her password and get into her phone to get to the bottom of it.

Shit. And to think I was close to letting Theo into my home.

I close my eyes, trying to concentrate. Theo and Amber might have met at the funeral, but aside from that, they have no connections aside from both knowing Stella. Could Stella have introduced them? And why would Theo need to tell Amber that he has Katy "in the palm of his hand." He even told her not to worry, like Amber had been in contact with concerns about my daughter.

Hot rage floods my veins. I can't trust Amber. I definitely can't trust Theo.

Now I need to work out if my daughter is in danger.

30

KATY

Checking my rearview mirror to make sure no one is behind me, I turn into the parking area at the trail-head and cut my lights. The sky is dark, with no moon, and I'm scared to leave the lit parking lot and go up the trail alone. But Theo said he would meet me up there. And I have a lot I need to talk about with him. I've found out some things he needs to know.

I'm alone at the trailhead, and the night is too dark for any nighttime hikers to be out. I pull out my phone, turn on the flashlight, and make my way across the lot to where the trail begins. I'm slow as I navigate, picking my way slowly up the path. All I can think of is how Mom died here, and maybe that happened because she rushed. I don't want to make the same mistake.

A voice sounds out through the shadows. "Katy, I'm here."

I turn the phone, and my light flashes over Theo. He's standing near the edge where Mom fell. I'm still careful as I cross the clearing. Theo reaches out and grabs me as I approach, pulling me into a hug. "I'm so glad you came. I thought your dad might stop you."

Suddenly, tears blind my eyes. I can't help myself, and I sob. Everything is just too much. I can't handle it anymore. It's not fair to ask someone my age to deal with everything that's been going on. I'm on the verge of collapsing to my knees when Theo catches me. I wrap my arms around him and sob into his shoulder. He rubs my back and makes soft shushing noises. I try to stop crying because I need to talk to him. He needs to know what I did.

"Hey, hey, it's okay. We're together now. Everything will be okay." His hands make circles across my back, soothing me.

Finally, I step back, still encircled by his arms. "I need to tell you something," I say, rubbing my nose.

"Tell me, then. You know you can tell me anything." Even though Theo is younger, he's taller and gazes down at me.

"Okay, okay, I'll tell you." I step away from him, forcing him to drop his arms.

We're just feet from the edge of the cliff, which makes me uncomfortable in the dark, so I move a few steps, and Theo follows.

"I... want to go to the police. I don't feel right about what we did."

His eyes flash in the dark. The night air between us becomes tense, like a piece of plastic stretched too thin.

"And why would you do that?" he asks.

"I don't feel right about lying." I take another step away from him, frightened by the low tone of his voice.

"You did it for me. Nothing wrong with protecting the people you care about." With every step I take back, he steps forward.

"But I lied... to the police, to my dad. What if they find out that I wasn't with you when your dad was murdered? Both of us could get in trouble." I sidestep again when he reaches out for me.

"We'll be fine as long as you don't tell anyone. You won't tell, will you?" His voice becomes high-pitched and wheedling, which bothers me. That tone makes me feel like a kid who has to be baby-talked into doing something.

"But I thought about it. I think we should go and tell the cops. You won't get in trouble because you didn't do it. And my dad will help us. I know he will. He has a great attorney. He's even trying to..." I stop, not sure how much I want to tell Theo.

"And why would your dad help me? I'm his dead wife's bastard kid." Theo turns away from me.

"No, listen." I reach out and place a hand on his shoulder. "My dad is trying to arrange it so that you can come live with us." When Theo turns around, I think he might be smiling although I can't see his face. "I heard my dad on the phone, with his attorney. He wants to do a DNA test."

"A DNA test for what?" Theo asks

"For you. To see if my dad is your dad. It could be true, you know. I mean, my mom and our dads..." I feel my face flush in the cool night air. "Uh, maybe she didn't know who your dad really was."

"Why the hell would I want something like that!" Theo yells at me, inches from my face. "Peter is not my damn dad! Andrew was my dad. That's the stupidest..." He stops, and his breathing grows harsher.

His hands slam into my shoulders, knocking me backward. My arms flail as I try to balance myself, to keep myself from falling over. *No, no, no,* my brain says. *You can't fall here, this is where she died.* I stumble but manage to keep myself upright. But now I realize there's more here to fear than a tumble over the side.

"Oh my god, Katy, I'm so sorry. I didn't mean to... I wouldn't hurt you." Theo advances on me, his hands held out.

I back away, trying to remember the direction of the cliff. I've gotten turned around in the darkness. I freeze when a branch snaps under my foot. I can't move again. I don't know if my next step will plummet me over the side, just like Mom. Theo still inches toward me. He grabs my hands and pulls me closer. I try to resist, but I'm scared that if he lets me go, I'll go flying and fall.

"I'm sorry, Katy, I swear. Listen, I'm not mad at you. I... I think I love you." Theo is breathless, his words coming out in a rush.

"What do you mean? Like, you love me like you loved your dad?"

He shakes his head and his thumbs gently stroke the backs of my hands. "No, not like that. Like I want you. Like I want to kiss you and touch you—"

"You can't!" I blurt out. "I'm your sister."

"Just my half sister." Theo tugs me closer.

My stomach churns.

"That's why you don't want the DNA test," I whisper. "Half or full, we're still brother and sister, Theo. It's wrong."

"Oh, come on, don't tell me you don't like me, too. I've seen the way you act around me. And all those texts... Were you just leading me on?"

He grips my hands more tightly, and I wince from the pressure and try to pull away. Theo leans forward, his breath on my face. After a few seconds, I register what's happening and turn my face just in time, and Theo's lips land on my cheek.

"Theo. Theo, please," I beg, trying to tug my hands away. "We can't. It's wrong."

"That's what Dad said when he saw our texts. But I don't care." He leans forward again and tries to kiss me. I twist, my wrists burning where his hands are wrapped tightly around them. "Rules are for morons, Katy. I learned that pretty early. We can do whatever we want. Stop trying to be the good girl." He leans in again. His grip tightens painfully.

"Ow. Theo, please, you're hurting me." I pull my arms back, trying to break his grip.

My heart thumps so hard that I feel it in my stomach. I'm scared, more scared than I've ever been. I didn't know Theo felt like this. And he scares me. I'm more than scared—I'm terrified. *Is Theo going to hurt me, throw me over the edge? Oh my God. Did Theo... Did he kill my mom, our mom? And his dad?* A whimper escapes me—I can't help it. Theo tries to pull me forward again. And I bring up my knee. It's the only thing I know to do. My mom always told me to go for the groin if a guy had me in his grip, so that's what I do. I knee Theo, and I knee him hard. And when he lets go with a loud groan, I run.

I plunge down the dark path, half running, half falling. I don't look back. Over the harsh rasp of my own terrified breathing, I can't tell if Theo is coming after me or not. But I keep running, tripping over rocks and pushing tree branches out of my face. I don't even stop to consider where the edge of the trail is. And finally, I burst into the parking area, the foggy lamplight illuminating my car on the far side. I'm almost free.

31

"Katy!" I call out, dashing up the stairs. "Katy, are you home?"

Please be home.

Losing Stella hurt me, but losing Katy would completely break me.

"Katy!" I stop at her bedroom door and knock. When she doesn't answer, I push on the door, expecting to find it locked again.

It opens, and the room is dark. Katy's not home.

"Where are you? Where are you?" I mutter to myself as I run back down the stairs.

I'm pretty sure she's with Theo. I have to find her. I have to know why Theo would say he has Katy in the palm of his hand. In the kitchen, I toss Amber's phone onto the counter and fish my phone out of my pocket. I dial Katy's phone, my leg jiggling nervously as I wait for it to go to voicemail. To my surprise, Katy answers.

"Daddy." She's out of breath, sounding like she's running. Her breathing is uneven and rapid in my ear. "Daddy," she says again.

"Katy, are you okay? Where are you?" My voice has a shrill edge to it, the beginnings of panic.

"Running. To my car," she pants in short bursts. "It's Theo."

Everything in me chills. "Where are you?"

"At the trail. Mom's trail." I hear her feet smacking the ground. Her breathing is labored and raspy again. "Theo's being weird. Daddy, I'm scared."

Forget chills—my heart freezes.

"Run, baby, run," I tell her. "Get to your car. Start driving. Get somewhere safe, and call me. I'm coming for you."

"Okay, Daddy." There's a sob in her voice.

"I'm going to start driving now, baby. Keep running. Daddy's coming." I turn and sprint from the kitchen to the stairs, taking them two at a time. "I'm coming, Katy. Run." The phone cuts out.

In the primary bedroom closet, on the opposite side of where I found Stella's hidden box, is a safe. It's tucked out of sight beneath my dress pants, clothes I hardly ever wear. Stella insisted on it, wanting somewhere to keep her good jewelry and important documents. And the gun she made me buy when we first moved into the house.

I never understood why she wanted a gun. We live in a safe neighborhood in an even safer city. Nothing has ever happened here that's made me remotely consider pulling that gun out of the safe. I haven't even thought about taking it out of the safe and cleaning it. Until now. I hope, if I need it, that it will fire. And I hope I don't need it.

I drop to my knees in the closet, scrambling to push aside the clothing hanging in my way. And as I fumble with the safe, I'm suddenly glad Stella insisted on a biometric lock. No way could I open a standard tumble lock right now. I press my thumb against the electronic pad on the front of the safe, and the door pops open. I move aside some paperwork and find the gun tucked underneath. After a quick check to make sure it's loaded with the safety on, I stand up, gun in hand, and run back down the stairs.

I leave the front door wide open and bolt down the drive, fumbling my keys and the gun until I finally manage to get in the car and get it started. Gun in my lap, I back down the driveway and turn my car in the direction of the mountain that my wife died on.

I drive as fast as I dare without getting pulled over, my attention alternating between watching the roads for Katy's car and checking the phone to see if she's calling. And that doesn't stop me from trying to figure out what's been going on. It's all a jumble in my head, a puzzle with missing pieces.

Why is Katy on the mountain with Theo? And why is Theo texting Amber? How is this all related? Would Theo really hurt Katy? Katy's terror tells me she thinks he will. I know so little about that kid. For all I know, he killed Stella. Fuck. And maybe Andrew, too. The thought makes me press my foot even harder on the gas. And all I can think about now is getting to my daughter.

I just hope I'm in time.

32

KATY

I'm almost to my car, almost safe. I see it a mere few yards away from me. I pat frantically at my pockets with my free hand, searching for my keys. I know they're here somewhere. The thought that I might have dropped them on the trail horrifies me, and I keep searching. I have to stop myself from crying out in relief when I find them in my jacket. They jingle loudly in the dark, and I know I'm giving away my whereabouts to Theo, but my ragged, harsh breathing and my pounding feet have probably done that anyhow. And I'm almost there.

The hit comes from one side. I didn't even realize Theo had somehow managed to bank around me and come at me from the opposite side of the car, but somehow, he managed. The body slam sends me flying, and my phone skitters out of my hand and lands somewhere beyond me in the dark. My knees dig into the gravel of the parking lot, the pain bursting hot across my legs. I scrabble to my feet, searching the darkness for *him*.

The lot is empty, with no other cars save mine and Theo's dad's truck—no night walkers or people coming to stargaze.

I'm alone with Theo. And Theo is crazy. That doesn't stop me from screaming. Who knows if someone is up the trail somewhere. Or someone might be passing by on the highway beyond the lot. If I scream loud enough, maybe someone will hear. I don't get the chance.

Theo reaches out and snatches my hair, pulling me down to the ground. I struggle against him, but the pain that radiates across my skull is blinding. All I do is thrash, my legs scraping against the ground as Theo drags me across the lot by my hair. I grunt, I cry, but he doesn't let me go. Even when I reach up and grasp his hands, it's no use—he won't let go, he's too strong.

I'm vaguely aware of the large boulder approaching us. He tosses me to the ground behind the rock and straddles me, one foot on either side of my body, trapping me on the sandy ground. I try to get my bearings, to figure out how far I am from the parking lot, but I can't think straight. When I whimper, he kneels and peers at me like he's studying a biology specimen.

"You know, Katy, this is going very differently than I pictured," he tells me. He reaches into his pocket, and when he brings his hand back out, he holds a large folding knife. With one flick, he opens it, and the wicked-looking blade winks in the phosphorus light of the streetlamps. "You were the only one I thought would understand."

The sight of the knife terrifies me. I can't help the sob that escapes from my lips. Fat tears blind me. I don't understand what Theo is talking about, but I need him to calm down.

"Explain it to me," I tell him as I try to swallow my sobs. "Make me understand what you're going through."

"Katy, dammit," he says softly, "I shouldn't have to explain it. I thought you were like me, like Mom. There's so few of us in the world, you know. People with our kind of darkness. I thought it was fate when I found out about you."

He still doesn't make sense. I try to inch backward, to free myself from under him, but he tuts at me and waves the knife.

"I wouldn't do that," he warns.

"Please, Theo, don't do this." Rocks bite into my back and scratch my hands. But as I stare up at Theo, I realize I might not make it out of here. The police might find my body in the same place they found my mother's.

"I'm not doing anything!" he shouts at me, spit flying. "But I'll explain it to you since you're evidently too stupid to figure it out yourself."

"Yes, tell me," I pant.

My heart batters against my ribs, and I'm afraid I'll pass out. But I've got to keep stalling him. Dad is on his way—he said so.

"We have the same mom—I don't know why you haven't figured this out. Anyhow," he says with the patient sigh of a teacher having to explain a lesson twice, "sweet Mom. She was dark, Katy. Maybe even darker than I ever realized. And I'm the same."

"No, Theo, you aren't dark. You're just... troubled," I say, using my dad's word.

"That's where you're wrong. There is are darkness in me. It eats at my insides. When I was younger, I tried really hard to be the perfect kid. I got good grades. I never got in any trouble. But then I found out about our mother. I found out what she was really like." Theo stands up and paces back and forth, still brandishing the knife.

"What do you mean?" Slowly, I inch myself backward, trying to keep Theo talking while moving away from him at the same time.

"I knew about you and your dad. Obviously. You know how little attention people actually give kids? It's like they think we can't hear or we won't understand what we're hearing. But I heard her on the phone with Peter and with you. I figured out what she was doing." He kneels down and grabs my ankle. "Don't move."

"Okay. Okay." I nod at him, my eyes wide.

"Anyhow," he continues, "I told her I knew about it. She didn't deny it. If anything, I think it made it more exciting for her."

"You think she liked the... excitement? That's why she did it?" I ask, almost softly. I'm not just keeping him talking now. I want to figure out Mom and why she did what she did.

"Oh yeah, of course she did. Her secret thrill came from convincing everyone she was a hard-working but loving wife and mother. That she had the perfect life and family. She managed to fool everyone, everyone except me." He resumes his pacing.

"What happened when you told her that you knew?" I ask.

"She denied it at first until I threatened to tell Dad. Then she confessed and offered me money. Whatever else she was, she was really good at her job. You have to be a good liar to be a pharmaceutical rep," he says with a barking laugh. "She didn't mind lying to doctors and patients, anything to make that money. So she had enough of it going around."

"I still don't understand why you're doing this." I sob again. *Where is Dad? What if he can't find me?*

"It's for you, Katy. Ever since I found out about you and followed you around, I knew you were like me, like our mom. You're the perfect girl for me. And I knew you'd understand me. And I understand you. There's no one like us, Katy." His voice is so calm, and he's so sure of himself that I'm terrified.

"We're supposed to be together. And I had to make sure that happened."

"Make sure? How? Did you do something?" Fear makes my words stick in my throat and I struggle to get them out, but I think I know now. Theo's unhinged. He's hurt people, and he's probably going to hurt me.

"Of course I did something." He laughs.

"Did you kill my mom?" The question comes out in a whimper. "I won't tell. I helped you before, remember?"

"Oh my God. I'm so tired of talking about her. And she's my mom, too." Theo stops his pacing and bends over me, waving the knife in front of my eyes. "Don't forget that. She was my mom, too."

"Did... did your dad cover for you?" Somehow, I always knew my mother's death wasn't an accident.

"Enough talking," Theo says. "I'm about done with this."

I throw up my arms to ward off the blow I know is about to come.

33

AMBER

Peter left quickly. I watched him from the peephole in the front door. He couldn't wait to get out of my house. Tonight didn't go exactly as I planned, but that's okay. I'm patient. I've been waiting a long time, and I can wait a little longer. He'll be wrapped around my finger before too long, then everything I've wanted will be mine. He's just got to get over the guilt. I'll help him realize that he doesn't have any reason to try to stay loyal to Stella's memory. She never cared about him. Or Katy. But I do.

After he's gone, I pad back into the living room and survey the room. It's in disarray, the cushions and pillows crumpled and askew. Thinking about why they look that way makes me smile. The plate with a few cookie remnants sits on the table with the two empty martini glasses. These I pick up and carry back into the kitchen, to load them into the dishwasher. Afterward, I straighten the sofa pillows. When I find my shorts stuffed between two cushions, I slide them on. That's when I realize something is missing. I glance around before it occurs to me. *My phone.*

I could've sworn I had it in here. I'm usually pretty careful about where I put my phone. I check the kitchen counter, thinking maybe I left it on the charger by accident. Not there. Back in the living room, I check the shelves near the television and under the coffee table, but I still don't see it. Frantically, I pull all the cushions off the sofa and search under each one, sliding my hands along the crevices, hoping to bump into the plastic case. Then it occurs to me—Peter didn't rush off because he felt guilty. He ran because he stole my phone. *But why?* I can only think of one reason. He saw something he shouldn't have.

Shit.

I rush to the bedroom, grab my laptop and set it up on the living room coffee table. I flip open the lid and pull up Whats-App, logging on so quickly that my fingers stumble over the keys. And there it is, my last message—from Theo. It would've shown up on my phone while Peter was here, probably while I was in the kitchen. And he saw it. And he stole my phone. While I'm fairly confident he won't be able to guess my passcode, it still makes me nervous. Any further messages from Theo will show up briefly on the home screen of the phone. Just a preview but enough to give him clues. No wonder he acted so weird.

I read the last couple of messages from Theo and get so angry that I could spit. He's going to screw up everything. I knew the kid was a loose cannon—he doesn't like to listen to anyone, much less an adult—but I thought I could keep him under control. I'm going to have to put a leash on that boy. He has no idea who he's messing with. Or how far I'll go to get what I want.

Luckily, I know exactly where to find him. I don't leave much to chance. I put a tracker on his dad's truck ages ago, when I realized he was taking it and sneaking out to meet up with Katy. I had to know where he was and what he was doing. So I created my way of keeping tabs on him. I swear if he messes this up, I'll wring his scrawny neck.

I pull up the tracker app and log in. When I see where he is, I cuss under my breath. Of course that's where he went. He's the most morbid kid I've met, obsessed with death, especially his mother's. The only other thing he's as obsessed with is Katy. Regardless, I've got to get there and get him under control before he ruins everything.

Without even bothering to change, I find my keys, check the tracker one more time, then head to my car. It's time to stop Theo once and for all.

34

KATY

The blow doesn't come. I lower my arms and peer up at Theo. He stands over me, knife in hand, but he doesn't strike at me.

"Theo?" The word comes out as a hoarse whisper. I don't want to startle him. "Theo, let me go. I won't say anything—I promise."

"You know," he says. His voice is loud in the darkness, "we could still work this out, you and I. The easiest thing to do is to go somewhere no one knows us. My dad always talked about heading to Mexico if he was ever running away from trouble. What do you think?"

"You... you want us to go to Mexico?" I ask numbly.

"We should have gone sooner, really. Before." I'm starting to think Theo isn't talking to me anymore, that he's just talking out loud.

"What do you mean, 'Before'?" I'm not even sure he hears me. "Before what?"

"Yeah, that's what we have to do. Start over. You and I." His smile is so disjointed and his words so divorced from reality that it makes me flinch.

He turns to me. "So what do you say, Katy. Katybug... Isn't that what your dad calls you? It's cute, like you. Katybug."

"Theo, listen. Yes, we'll... we'll go, you and I. But we'll find my dad. He'll help us. He wants to help you." I beg him now. "Please, Theo."

"Ha!" Theo turns on me again. "Your dad is just as bad as mine. Maybe I should take care of him, too."

My blood chills. "Theo, did you hurt... your dad?" I know the answer before he even tells me.

How could I have been so stupid? I've been hanging out with Theo for weeks now, sneaking out of my house, lying to my dad. Theo's crazy. Theo's a killer.

"Mm, yeah," he responds with something like a giggle. "Had to. He knew about us and was going to tell your dad. He tried to keep us apart. But he couldn't. Here we are, just the two of us."

"And Mom?" I ask, my heart squeezing so hard I think it's going to burst. "Did you... Oh God. Theo, did you hurt my mom?"

"*Our* mom. Jesus, how many times do I have to remind you of that? She was *our* mom. But no, Katybug, I did not kill our mom." He crouches beside me and reaches out, smoothing my hair away from my tearstained face. "Mom would understand about you and I. I wouldn't hurt her. I'm too much like her."

"I don't believe you," I say in a shivering whisper. Gulping back my tears, I stare defiantly up at Theo. "You're just saying that because you know I'd never be with the person who killed my mother."

I kick out at him, catching his shin. He stumbles but doesn't fall.

"You going to kill my dad, too?"

Theo is quiet, rubbing his shin, his face thoughtful. I wish

I knew what was going on behind his cold eyes. Quiet Theo scares me even more than ranting Theo. I whimper and scoot backward in the dirt.

"Theo, we'll never be together. Listen to me," I say when he shakes his head, "I hate you, Theo. There will never be an *us*."

He strikes like a snake, raising the knife as I scramble to one side, trying to kick at him and move at the same time. He plunges the knife downward.

White-hot pain explodes across my leg, and I scream. Then I scream again when Theo wrenches the knife from my thigh. Slick heat bubbles up and streams across my leg, so warm I smell it in the night air, coppery and salty all at once. My vision blurs. I blink, trying to see Theo through the thick tears that stream from the corners of my eyes.

"Theo," I whimper.

"Now, you're just something else I have to take care of. You were supposed to be the one, Katy."

His outline shifts dimly as he raises the knife again. I roll, gritting my teeth at the pulling pain in my leg.

Theo grunts, and I hear a clatter. The knife—he dropped it. I wrench my good leg underneath myself and, pushing, manage to get to my feet. I hear Theo scrambling around in the dirt. I don't even look at him. With a grunt, I stumble, almost falling when my injured leg buckles, but I keep going. Screaming as I run, I hope someone has pulled into the parking lot or someone on the highway hears me. I just know I have to keep running.

But I'm not fast enough to outrun a crazed fifteen-year-old boy. He tackles me from behind, and we both crumple to the ground, and I feel a fresh spurt of hot blood wet my leg. Theo tugs my hair, slapping me, trying to get his hands around my throat. But I fight back. I feel a thrill of triumph when my fingers score his cheeks, leaving marks down his face. He grunts, and I claw his face again, trying to find his eyes, to plunge my fingers into the soft sockets.

A shot rings out, a reverberating crack.

Theo jumps off me, and I see a man's silhouette next to a new vehicle in the lot. My heart soars. Dad. Come to rescue me. Come to save my life.

And then I see the gun in his hand pointed at Theo.

Is he going to pull the trigger?

For a millisecond, I want to let him. But Theo isn't hurting me anymore. If Dad shoots and kills him now, it might get him in trouble.

I can't lose my dad, not after everything that has happened.

"Daddy, no!" I scramble to my knees and manage to get to my feet. I'm bloody and broken, skin lacerated on the rocks and pain radiating all over my body. But I run—to my daddy.

Theo takes off in the opposite direction. Dad raises his gun.

"Don't do it." I put my hand on his and force him to lower the weapon. Instead, he pulls out his phone and calls 911. Then, we climb into the car, lock the doors, and wait for the police to come.

35

AMBER

Of all the places to go, of course he's on the trail where his mother died. And I bet Katy is with him. I try to think of what to tell them when I see them, what to say when Katy asks me why I'm out on the mountain at night. I'll think of something. Katy is such a sweet, trusting girl. She'll believe anything I say. I've been her Aunt Amber for years now, practically another mother. She'll believe me before she'll believe Theo.

I speed across town and take the turnoff toward the trail, but as I'm about to pull into the parking area, I see them sitting in a car. I stop in a pullout and cut my lights, not wanting Peter or Katy to notice me. I don't see Theo anywhere, but his dad's truck is still parked on the far side of the lot. I can't stay here. No doubt, the police are on their way.

I back away from the lot entrance and turn around, hoping that Peter and Katy are distracted enough to not notice my car. Peter can't know I was here. He can't know how I knew to come here. I head home again.

Not knowing where Theo is, I keep an eye out, expecting to see him around every turn I make. A couple of miles out, I pass two police cars and an ambulance headed toward the mountain parking lot. As I pass, I hope my car is nondescript enough not to stand out.

My fingers tighten around the steering wheel. Maybe it's time to bow out. I never should have trusted that kid and now I know for sure what a loose cannon he is.

The question is—will he now come after me?

I don't know what to do. All I know is that I will do everything in my power to make sure I come out on top as always.

36

Dear Mom,

I don't know what to do. Nothing is going right for me. I thought everything was going to work out the way I needed it to, but now I'm not sure. I don't like feeling this way. I feel so lost, even more than before.

I'm beginning to question myself, and I don't like the way it feels. Sometimes, I wish you were still alive. Isn't that crazy? I hate you and I was glad I killed you but sometimes I regret it. Only you could make me feel that way. I guess it's true what they say about the maternal bond with your children being complicated. So many different emotions—I've loved you and hated you all at the same time. Wanted your attention and wanted you gone. Wanted to be you and wanted to be with you. I feel so alone without you now. I wish I could talk to you again. Wish you could help me figure out what to do. All I ever wanted was the perfect family, and I thought I found it.

But it's slipping through my fingers.

37

The ambulance bumps along the highway, and I hold tight, swaying back and forth on a bench bolted to the vehicle wall. Katy is strapped into a stretcher, a bright red spot blooming on the white sheets covering her. Her face is scratched and bleeding and a lump is bruising on her forehead. But she's awake, alert. She reaches over and grasps for my hand. I take hers and squeeze tightly, not letting go until we reach the hospital emergency room and the paramedics roll her away into the unit.

I follow behind as quickly as possible and wait just on the other side of the curtain divider while the doctors stitch up her leg and treat a laceration on her arm. A nurse offers me a cup of coffee while I wait for the doctors to finish up. When they finally pull the curtain back, Katy is dozing on a hospital bed, dressed in a clean gown and covered with a blanket.

"Let's let her rest for a minute, Mr. McConnell," Dr. Lee tells me. She's maybe forty, with jet black hair peppered by the occasional gray. Since we arrived, she's felt like a calm presence and knowing my daughter is in safe hands makes this painful process slightly better.

"Yeah, okay." I step away but not so far that I still can't see Katy. I'll probably never let her out of my sight again.

"Katy is going to be fine." Dr. Lee flips through her chart. "All of her wounds are superficial. She's young. Everything will heal fine. There will be a scar on her leg, but if that really worries her, I can put you in touch with the plastic surgery department at some point. She needs some rest."

"Okay. Anything I should worry about?" I ask.

"Well, Katy has just been through something very traumatizing. We need to make sure that Katy has a strong support system. That's going to include a therapist, possibly a psychiatrist. And, of course, her dad." The doctor reaches over and clasps my shoulder. "And how is Dad?"

"Uh, fine. I'm fine. Katy is the one who was hurt."

"Physically, yes, but a shock like you've had can do funny things to a person. Let me have the nurse take your vitals, at least. I'll send her back in to do it. You can stay here with Katy."

"Yeah, okay. As long as I can stay here with Katy, you can do whatever you need to. I'm just not leaving Katy."

"Excellent. I'll send the nurse in. And what about the police? They'll want to speak with you as well." Dr. Lee makes a few notes in Katy's chart while she's talking.

"I can talk to them when they're ready. But let's wait a while before we let them talk to Katy."

"Daddy?" Katy's voice is hoarse, making me forget about the doctor as I rush to her side.

I pour a cup of water from a nearby pitcher and offer her the plastic cup. She takes it and sips, nodding.

"I'm okay, Daddy, I promise."

"I know, Katybug. I know."

I sit on the chair next to the bed and take her hand in mine. It seems so small, its bones fragile and tender.

"Everything is going to be okay. The doctors are taking good care of you."

"I'm sorry. I never should have been out there with Theo. He's been... He's not good. He's just not." Tears overspill and roll down her scratched cheeks.

"Hey, no, no. None of this is your fault. You have nothing to apologize for." I squeeze her hand reassuringly. "We can move past this."

"But the things he said... Dad, he killed Andrew. And you almost went to jail for it." Katy winces as she shifts on the bed. "And he knew about us all this time. He knew Mom had a second family."

"He knew? How?" This news confounds me. "He knew everything?"

"He heard her on the phone—I guess with you. He managed to put it together." She sips her water, wetting her lips. "I think... I think that he, you know, caused mom's accident." Big tears drop onto her hospital gown, leaving splotches behind. She rubs her nose, sniffling. "And he said the craziest things. About how he had a darkness in him and that he was just like Mom."

"Well, I think there's no denying that," I remark.

A nurse enters the room, a stethoscope around her neck, and checks my vital signs. I hold out an arm willingly while Katy keeps talking.

"He wanted us to be together." She glances at the nurse. "You know, like *together* together. I tried to tell him how wrong that was, but he had... his own ideas." Katy shudders.

I have to keep myself from flinching. Andrew was right, at least about Theo's intentions. And I'd been wrong about something: Theo wasn't troubled—he was downright disturbed. And I'd tried to bring him into my home, into my family. I thought I could help him. More likely, we all would have wound up hurt or worse. Theo needs the kind of help I can't give.

Tears flow freely down Katy's face. She's given up trying to be brave. "He's hurt so many people, Dad. The police have to catch him, or I'm afraid you'll be next."

"They will, honey. They will. He's not going to get away with any of this."

Just as I reassure Katy, someone knocks at the door, and we both turn to see Detective Anderson in the doorway.

"Hope everyone is okay," he tells us. "Can I come in?"

I look at Katy for confirmation before nodding and waving him in.

He stands at the end of the bed, his arms crossed over his chest. "You feel like talking any, young lady?"

"You don't have to if you aren't ready," I tell Katy quickly.

"No, I want to." Katy's jaw flexes and I see new determination glint like steel in her eyes. "Have you caught him yet?"

"I'm sorry, but we haven't," he replies. "I've got a patrol out, canvassing the area. We'll find him."

Katy grips my hand, and I feel her trembling, and I know what she's thinking. She's not safe. We're not safe, not while Theo is still out there.

38

AMBER

After pulling into the driveway, I bolt from the car to the door, almost dropping my keys as I try to fit one into the keyhole. My hands shake. I have to get out of here. I have to leave town and start over. I knew it as soon as I saw Peter and Katy at the trailhead tonight.

Theo is still out there somewhere and I'm not safe, not with him around. I have to leave and go somewhere he can't find me. No one has ever terrified me like Theo—not Stella, not even myself.

Once I manage to pry the door open, I dash to my bedroom and pull a duffel bag from the closet. I cram clothes into the bag, not really paying attention to what I'm packing. That doesn't matter to me. Along with the clothes, I add a couple of notebooks and a few photos I have. To me, they're the most important things I own. With the bag stuffed full, I zip it closed and fling it over my shoulder, glancing around my room one more time in case I've forgotten something important. I wish I still had my phone, but I'll just buy a burner somewhere once I'm safe. I'll call Peter from there and maybe try to explain everything to him. I can't let him go without some sort of explanation, some kind of closure.

As fast as I can, I make a sweep of the living room and kitchen, remembering that just a few hours earlier, I was entwined with Peter, right there on my sofa. A few hours ago, I thought everything was perfect. I thought everything was going to work out. I thought my plan had worked. I thought I had what I wanted.

What I want now is to get away from here before Theo shows up. And he will, eventually.

With my duffel bag in hand, I hurry across the hall and out the front door. I don't bother stopping to lock it. *Who cares now?* I pull open my car door and sling the bag inside. But when I look for the keys in my pocket, I realize I don't have them. I left them inside, having dropped them on the table by the entryway. Panic has made me careless. Cursing, I sprint back to the house.

The keys aren't where I thought I left them. I make a quick sweep of the kitchen, searching the countertops before I head into the bedroom. Maybe I dropped them while I was packing. I search the bed, shifting pillows and comforters, before I turn to the closet. It's the only other place they can be. *Did I close the closet door like that?*

Fear prickles across the back of my neck, and I stop, my hand on the closet doorknob. I swallow thickly, not wanting to open the door. *Your mind is playing tricks on you,* I tell myself. But something tells me not to open that door. I drop my hand and step back. No way are the keys in there. And I did shut the door. Maybe I left the keys in the lock. People do that. I walk backward, keeping an eye on the closet. When the door stays shut, I sigh with relief and turn to leave the bedroom.

A soft squeak stops me. I hear a shuffle, the quiet sound of a sneaker on a hardwood floor, and a metallic jingle. I turn slowly, holding my breath.

Theo is standing in my bedroom. My car keys dangle from his fingers.

"Looking for these?" He holds them out and jangles them at me.

I turn and run.

Behind me, I hear the sound of the keys hitting the floor. Then a heavy weight crashes into my back, sending me flying through the door into the hallway.

"You messed everything up, Amber." His breath is hot in my ear.

"Theo, no. Things aren't messed up. We can still make this work," I pant, my pulse pounding.

He pushes my head down into the carpet. "Then why were you running? You think you can leave without me?"

"I was going to come find you. Really, I was. So we could leave together." My voice is high and imploring but muffled against the carpet. "I wasn't going to leave without you. I promise."

"You think I'd leave with you?" he asks with a barking laugh. "Nope, I'm on my own now."

"We're still a team, Theo. Remember our plan." I try to turn my head to face him but his grip is too tight. "Come on. Let's go. We can talk everything over in the car."

"I'm not going anywhere with you!" he screams in my ear "You. Ruined. Everything." I feel the sharp point of a knife against my ribs.

"No," I sob. "Don't do this!"

Desperate, I squirm under his weight, pulling myself an inch or so along the floor with my fingernails. He grabs my hair and pulls so hard it feels like my scalp is coming away from my skull. But when I scream as loud as I can, his other hand, the one with the knife, clamps over my mouth. The plastic handle of the knife becomes slick with my saliva. When I bite into his palm, he drops it.

Now I manage to twist my body around so that I see his beetroot-red face. I lift a hand and punch him on the nose. I'm not the strongest woman in the world but it's enough to make him jerk back. Theo's eyes are crazed, wide, his pupils almost entirely black. I wriggle out from under him and dash down the hallway, heading for the stairs.

He slams into my back and I go flying, falling against the wall and tripping over my feet. But as I spin, and am about to tumble down the stairs, my fingers find purchase on Theo's shirt, pulling him with me.

We're a tangle of limbs as we bump down the stairs. And then we both land at the bottom of the staircase, winded and bruised. I think I may have broken a rib and possibly my ankle judging by the throbbing pain emanating from both.

Groaning, I crawl across the floor, aiming for the kitchen door. Theo's hand wraps around my ankle and tugs at me. My fingers reach for the doorframe and brush against the edge, but I can't quite reach it. I stretch again, and this time, my hand finds and clasps the doorjamb, and I pull myself through into the kitchen. My legs scrambling beneath me, I finally manage to pull myself to my feet, wincing at the pain. I dash around the counter and grab a knife from the block.

"You killed my mother, Amber!" he screams. "Now, it's your turn!" He rips the toaster from the plug and lunges at me.

I push out my hand and sense the knife finding Theo's torso. And at the same time, the toaster smashes into my temple. My body crumples and I fall sideways. In one last twist of fate, my temple hits the kitchen counter on the way down. But as the knife clatters to the tiles, I see the blood on the blade and smile.

"Ow," Theo says, staring at the blood seeping from his wound.

The world turns black around the edges, but I'm glad I get to see him drop to the kitchen floor.

He reaches for me. "You killed her. You killed Stella."

"Yes," I whisper, as the world goes black.

I did kill her.

And then my thoughts drift to Peter. A man who deserved better than my lying mother. A man who should have been mine, and who almost was.

Peter.

39

"I, Amber Sears, devise and bequeath all my property, both real and personal, to the following persons: Peter McConnell and Katy McConnell." David lowers the paper and looks across the desk at us. "She left it all to you, both of you. The house and its contents, all accounts, and a rather large life insurance policy."

He slides the paper across the desk, and I pick it up and read the first paragraph of the will.

"Did she say why?" I return the paper and lean over to Katy, putting an arm across her shoulders.

She smiles sadly at me and pats my hand.

"I don't know. Guilt, maybe?" David shrugs and shuffles through the stack of papers in front of him.

"Amber loved us, Dad, in her own way," Katy says softly. "And with everything that's happened, does it really matter why? Let's just sell the houses and get out of this town. Let's go somewhere no one knows us. I'll finish school there."

"Is that what you want?" I ask.

She nods. "Maybe we could move closer to Gran."

"Okay." I pat my daughter's knee. "I like that idea. It'll be nice to be around family again. David, can you help us arrange everything? Get any paperwork that we need started?" I'm ready to put everything behind us, too. I just wish I could get answers to certain questions.

"I guess we're just going to have to move on without any answers, right? We'll never know why Theo and Amber were in communication," Katy says, practically reading my mind.

"Closure would be nice, but you're right." I sigh.

I never did get into Amber's phone. In fact, I tried to guess the passcode so many times that it eventually permanently locked me out. And with both Theo and Amber gone—after killing each other in a bizarre twist of fate—we'll never be able to ask them. I need to find a way to be okay with that somehow. Katy is safe now, though. Yes, she has scars from that night, physical and psychological, but we'll work through those eventually. Her safety is all that matters now. I just need to forget about the why and concentrate on the now. At least, that's what my therapist told me.

* * *

I have to shove on the door with my shoulder to get it open. And when I do, I'm almost sorry I opened it. No one has been at Amber's house in months. I gag slightly at the smell. It's thick and rusty, and I know immediately what it's from. I press my hand across my nose and step into the house. It's quiet, not even the hum of a refrigerator breaking the silence.

In the middle of the kitchen floor is the stain. It spreads from one side to the other, dried to a brown rust. I find spatters of dried blood on the countertop and cabinets. A coating of black dust, fingerprint powder, covers most of the surfaces. And the spot where Amber's toaster once sat, is empty. I stand and stare at the stains and suddenly can't stand them being there anymore.

In the laundry room, I find a bucket, sponges, and cleaning liquid. I make up a bucket of soapy water and get to business, starting in the kitchen. Wiping and scrubbing, changing the water in the bucket whenever it turns brown, I move across the floor, cleaning up footprints I know are Amber's. I wind up on my knees in the hallway. Tears spatter the floor, mixing in with the bloody spots. I clean and clean until the stains are gone and the smell finally subsides.

I don't stop there. I open the refrigerator and sweep all the contents into a garbage bag then tie it up and dump it in the outside bin. I walk through the house, dusting and cleaning. I ignore the sofa, unwilling to think about the last time I was on it. But room by room, I clean, trying to put Amber's memory to rest.

In a small alcove Amber had set up like an office, I find her laptop. Curious, I open the lid. I'm not surprised to find it passworded. I give it several tries, trying to guess her password. Like the phone, whatever information is on her laptop is lost to me. I set it aside and straighten a stack of papers on her desk. I feel like I'm violating Amber's trust, invading her privacy, but technically, everything in this house belongs to me, including a photo album I find tucked into the bottom drawer of her desk.

I sit at the desk and flip through the album, smiling at the pictures of a young Amber. Then I notice something. The pictures are only Amber—no family, no siblings, no father, no mother. Just Amber. And in so many of them, she's not smiling. I notice the series of houses in the background changes frequently, and something suddenly dawns on me. Amber was a foster child. She appears to have moved from home to home. As the pictures progress, Amber becomes more sullen, more withdrawn looking and, somehow, more familiar.

The last page of the album has no picture. Instead, a newspaper clipping is paperclipped to the edge of the page. I pull it off, the paper brittle with age, and read the headline: "Newborn Found Abandoned." The article goes on to explain how a newborn baby girl was found on the steps of the local hospital. A photo has been inserted at the bottom of the article, and everything suddenly clicks.

The picture in Stella's closet, the one I found in the secret box, is *Amber*. Amber is the baby in the article.

I paw through the rest of Amber's papers, piecing together her life before we knew her. And everything I learn sends a shockwave through me. *Amber*. My God! Everything comes back to her. And now it all makes sense. Amber was Stella's daughter. I don't need a DNA test to tell me that. I look back through the album, noting the resemblance of young Amber to Katy. And Amber might have dyed her hair when I knew her, but when she was young, it was the same auburn shade as Stella's.

I quickly do the math between Stella's age and Amber's and realize Stella couldn't have been more than fifteen at the time—so young to go through so much. She must've hidden the pregnancy from her parents and given birth somewhere alone before abandoning the baby. Maybe that was the reason Stella was the way she was—trauma from her youth. Or maybe, like Theo said, she was carrying a darkness of her own.

While I'm on the floor, surrounded by pieces of Amber's life, I find the most shocking thing of all, a letter. And it starts with, "Dear Mom."

EPILOGUE

Dear Mom,

I remember the last time I saw you, standing there on the edge of the cliff, mouth wide open, unable to believe what I was saying. I used to love our hikes. Back when I thought you could be a good person. I loved having something that only you and I did, something just for us. And I thought it would be the perfect place for me to finally tell you, for you to find out who I was.

I was so scared to tell you. It's why I hid it for so, so long. You left me before, when I was just a baby. What was to stop you from leaving me now? And I always wondered if, one day, you'd look over at me and realize that I was your daughter, but you never did. So I had to tell you that day. I wish you'd just known. You're my mom. How could you not know your own child?

Do you have any idea what you did to me? Being in the foster care system is horrible—shunted around from one family to another, never knowing what kind of family you're going into. And I've been with some pretty bad ones. Shared a room with seven other kids, had food locked up and kept away from me, used as unpaid domestic labor. And there was other stuff, too, stuff too bad to mention here, stuff I try to forget. And it was all because of you, because you just left me lying outside a hospital, wrapped in a blanket. I hate you for that.

So I confronted you. Right there, on the mountain, with the cliff drop in front of us, the lower trail running below it.

You said you were only fifteen. Do you think that excuses your actions? "My boyfriend pressured me to have sex." You wouldn't believe some of the things I've been pressured into doing.

You told me you didn't know you were pregnant. You thought it was weight gain from drinking a lot. Am I supposed to feel sorry for you because you gave birth in a gas station bathroom? At least you had the sense to steal a baby blanket from the stroller parked outside. And thanks for dropping me off at the hospital, I guess. At least you didn't dump me in the trash or try to flush me down the toilet. You know what? I almost felt sorry for you when you told me how you had to stop in a cemetery on the way and deliver the afterbirth.

Oh, I don't care that you went home alone and

cried yourself to sleep. So what if your parents weren't home a lot. At least you had parents! You think being vaguely neglected gives you reason to lie and steal? To cheat and manipulate? You did all that just so someone would pay attention to you.

Where was my attention? Where was the love for me? Poor abandoned me.

And even after all that, all your lies and deceit, you still wound up with the perfect family, Peter and Katy. How did you get so lucky? You wasted the time you could have had with them by running back and forth between them and Andrew and Theo. You wound up with two families. Two! So selfish, having two families to yourself when I had none. You didn't deserve any of them. And then you wanted me to keep your secret. Selfish to the very end.

If I had to pick, I wouldn't have chosen the death that you had. Pushing you off that cliff was impulsive. You'd made me so angry. All I wanted was for us to go to Peter and tell him the truth, tell him who I was. I could have been part of the family then. I could have been a big sister to Katy. And I was scared, listening to your screams. I was sure someone was going to come running or that someone had seen what I did. Somehow, no one saw me. I kept waiting on the police to show up at my house, for them to come and arrest me, but it never happened. That's when I knew I could get what I wanted. If it hadn't been for Theo.

Let me tell you, that kid is just like you. He's a

lying, sneaking, conniving little bastard. But it was my fault. I wasn't careful enough around him. He caught me watching him and his dad one day. Said he'd seen me before. I never would have told him who I was, but the kid pulled a knife on me! I never counted on Theo, but he's come in handy, especially with Katy. I don't like the kid, but he's inherited your devious mind. That was the plan we made: Peter for me and Katy for Theo. Sure, I thought it was twisted, you know, with all the incest, but what did I care? You've done far worse, Mom.

And now, here we are. You're gone, and I'm still here. I'll be the mother to Katy she should have. I'll be the wife that Peter deserves. I might even be able to help Theo. I can be there for them when they need me, not like you. I'll be everything that you weren't. And thanks to you, I'll finally have my family

I'm going to be happy, Mom. Just you watch me.

Your Daughter,
Amber

* * *

Thank you for reading THE SECRET FAMILY. If you enjoyed this book please consider leaving a review, they are so useful for other readers and help authors so much.

ABOUT THE AUTHOR

Even as a young child SL Harker would conjure up stories to share with her family. That love of books and storytelling never went away, but her skills have improved since then.

As a lover of twisty fiction, her books are fast-paced domestic thrillers with a little spice added in.

ALSO BY SL HARKER

The New Friend

The Work Retreat

The Bad Parents

The Nice Guy

The Secret Family

Made in United States
Orlando, FL
19 August 2023

36247945R00121